The Vase: Change of Fate

By
Amber Turner Darby

Editor: Shari Armstrong

Interior Designer: Tony Bradford

Exterior Designer: Robert King

ISBN: 978-1-938950-44-5

Greater Is He Publishing
9824 E. Washington St.
Chagrin Falls, Ohio 44023
Phone: 216.288.9315
www.GreaterIsHePublishing.com

Acknowledgements

Thank you God, for giving me life and the gifts and talents that I have. Thank you Mom and Dad, for supporting my dreams and loving me. Thank you Riverdale Baptist School for helping me conquer my challenges and discover my talents. Thank you Dr. Mike and DeeDee Freeman, my Pastors at Spirit of Faith Christian Center for your teachings. Thank you Deidra Bell, Jhonna Brookins, and Xemena Thomson, for being my greatest friends. Have fun in college.

Dedication

To my Mom and Dad. Thank you for loving me for who I am and supporting me, from my upcoming future to my craziest ideas. You two have always been there for me and even though I don't say it enough, I appreciate and I love you both. Don't celebrate too much when I go to college, okay?

CONTENTS

Chapter 1:

The Great Past

Long ago, there was peace. Then, there was a war, a great war between two great Kingdoms. One was Arigog, the land of red, glory, and honor. The other was Destera, the land of purple, strength, and loyalty. As the war went on in the lands, a change came over Arigog: Vases.

The Vases were small sculptures that told of one event happening in the owner's future and were made by a small group who called themselves Foretellers. But not many people paid attention to them because they knew that the war was more important.

During this time, both heroes and enemies rose in the lands. One famous hero, William Asselin, fought for the land of Arigog. In the prime of his youth, however, great news was brought to the land: Dain, the King of Destera, was pronounced dead, and the fighting ceased. The Destramechs never surrendered or continued to fight; they just stopped and went quiet. As a result, the war ended.

As the desire for battle decreased, the change of life in Arigog increased. Without a war to be a distraction, the Vases increased as they became a new way of life. As time progressed, more Foretellers came into existence. The most famous was Madame Leona, a Foreteller who made Vases that foretold entire lives.

Through her, Arigog became an isolated and civilized land, closing themselves completely off from the outside world. They stopped their desires for honor, glory and everything that would make a person Arigogian, and instead increased a desire for perfection and etiquette. But as their land experienced peace, the world began to suffer.

Now, the lands have been blinded in darkness. How long, once again, will it take for the world to see the light?

Chapter 2:

The Baby Princess

It was a beautiful dawn. The golden sun was beginning to shine in the sky, glowing on the lovely mansions and angel-sculpted roads below as people began to gather and parade up a long hill. This crowd, mostly containing large families, was dressed in their most civilized forms of clothing. The men were dressed in blue clothes while the women were in pink dresses. Some of the women had their arms linked to their husbands'. Others were holding an infant or the hands of their little ones. But all had smiles on their faces and their heads held high with pride as they showed off their children like trophies. The children had polished faces, and their teeth were as white as the clouds above them. They too were dressed like their parents, in fancy clothes and uniform dresses while the infants were wrapped in their blankets and held in their mothers' arms.

A father with his family looked around at all the people around him. Then, looking in a particular direction, he directed his family over to another family nearby.

"Wonderful morning, Peter," announced the father. The other father looked in the direction of the source and smiled.

"Why, George, good to see you again, and yes, it is a wonderful morning indeed."

"I am truly sure that you are as excited as I am for this lovely event."

"Indeed," replied Peter. "It is not every day that a baby of the royal family is born, and on such a lovely day, too. What did they say that the child is to be?"

"A girl," George said. "And they also say that she is extremely beautiful. The most beautiful baby girl that many have seen in a very long time."

"Really? You think that she may take the throne?"

"She might. If she is as beautiful as rumored and if it is foretold on her Vase, I am sure the throne will be hers. After all, only the most beautiful women that have been foretold are chosen for the throne." With a reassuring smile, George turned his head forward, continuing to keep his wife's arm locked with his. Peter returned a smile and did the same.

The parade continued to climb up the hill until they had reached the destination. Up on top of the hill was a beautiful white castle with a red roof, giant wooden doors and a moat drawbridge. As people entered the opened palace, a long hall awaited them. At the end of the hall were two more large, old, and wooden doors.

Boom!

The doors opened to a large throne room with large red banners on the walls. On one side of the room were servants, and on the other side were maids, standing tall and ready to await orders.

At the end was the royal family on their thrones with the portly King in the middle and a large red banner of a yellow dragon above them. The King, like his family, was brown-haired, he had brown eyes and his beard was short and trimmed. On the King's left was his wife, whose blue eyes and beautiful face were shining for all to see. On his right were his children, sitting properly on their thrones. And there in the Queen's arms was the baby girl. Her large brown eyes were perfectly matching her faint rosy cheeks and brown hair.

When as many people as could fit entered the room, the servant closest to the throne stepped forward and shouted,

"Presenting the royal family of Arigog!" An applause broke out and died almost as quickly as it came. The servant continued, "First, presenting King William of Arigog!" The crowd bowed to the King. "Presenting Queen Barona of Arigog, mother of young Princess Katelyn and Prince Andrew of Arigog!" The crowd bowed again to the Queen, three-year-old Katelyn, and four-year-old Andrew. "And finally, presenting the newest member of the family: The royal baby girl, Princess Amelia of Arigog!" The crowd bowed and applause came, this one much louder and longer than the other one. "And now, if you would move to the ballroom, a feast is held in celebration of the new child. The King will be there to join you all shortly." The second this was announced, the crowd turned around and went out of the throne room, and half of the servants and maids went to join them, closing the large doors and leaving the royal family to themselves.

"Nicely done, if I do say so myself," said William with a smile to the servant, who was setting himself with the others.

Boom!

The doors opened again as four men in red cloaks entered the room. "Ah! Elders, you all have made it. It is good to see you all. I thought I did not see any of you with the rest of the crowd."

"It is good to see you too, my King," said an Elder in the middle. "Forgive us. We do not like to be around the common folk, for we prefer to make our businesses a bit more personal." They all bowed, and then he stepped forward and said, "My, the child is truly beautiful."

"Indeed," replied another Elder, "You think she will have the throne?"

"Well, we will not know about anything for this infant until her Vase is completed. I am sure Madame Leona would at least have the visions and start today. Where is she, anyway? Has she already seen you, my King?"

"You do not have to worry about me," said a slow and calm voice, "I am right here. And her Vase is already completed. I had been having visions about her whole life when the Queen was with child."

Everyone turned around as a blonde-haired lady in blue robes entered. Behind her were several servants pushing a cart that had the Vase. It was a large, sculpted vase, painted with small, square-shaped pictures as if a timeline and finished with a shining polish.

"Splendid!" announced William. "Now that you and her Vase are here, interpret to us what it means for my daughter's life. Just the important parts we really need to know about."

"Of course, Your Majesty," replied Madame Leona with a curtsey. Then, she went to the Vase and placed her finger on the first small painting: a small baby wrapped in white blankets, shining as if it was the sun. "Let us see . . . the child will be born a happy and healthy girl. From the day that she is born, she will be extremely beautiful for all to see. And she will be the one to take the throne."

"Finally," said an Elder, "I was beginning to fear that the land would never see its next ruler."

Leona moved her finger past several pictures until she stopped on one of a small girl in a little pink dress. "She will begin to develop as an obedient and happy child." She then skipped many pictures until she stopped on a yellow painting. This was of the girl, now older, holding hands with a blonde haired boy on one knee, both smiling. In the blue painting next to it, the two are holding hands, the boy dressed in red and the girl in a long white dress. "Ah, yes," Leona started, "A celebration will be held to celebrate the day that she is a woman at the age of twenty. There, a blonde-haired man will have the King's blessing and will ask the girl for her hand in marriage. The girl will happily say yes, and they will get married the next day."

"*Eeeeeek!*"

A maid had squealed and jumped with joy, grabbing everyone's attention. Leona pretended as if she did not hear it and continued, moving her finger toward another painting. This was of the couple wearing crowns and surrounded by children.

"They will have many children as the King steps down and they take their places on the thrones. Then, the husband will rule as king with the princess by his side, as he brings peace to all the lands." She then went down to the last four paintings: a green skull, a coffin, a fire, and a Vase. "The princess will grow old, die of a sudden disease, and will have a lovely funeral. Then, her body will be burned and her ashes will be put into her Vase."

"Just like mine," said Katelyn, pointing her finger at herself with a big smile on her face.

"Of course it is, Daughter," Barona replied, "Everyone wants to be put into their Vase when they die." She smiled at Katelyn, who in return, smiled back.

William then stood up. "Well then, if that is all, I shall now be attending the feast. Good day." And with that, the King left the room with the rest of the servants and maids behind him.

Chapter 3:

The Naughty Children

"Do not do it, Brother." Andrew, Katelyn, and six-year-old Amelia crept down the hall and peeked behind a wall. A maid was next to a curtained window, scrubbing the floors. "I am not sure what you are about to do, but you should not try to do it, Brother." said Amelia.

"She is right, Brother," said Katelyn, "We should focus on other things."

"It will be quick, Sisters. Do not worry."

They stood there hidden for several minutes. While waiting, Amelia felt as if someone was behind her; she turned around and jumped. A girl Amelia's age with brown hair and a simple face stood. "You have scared me, Mary."

"I am sorry, Princess," Mary whispered. "What are you all doing?"

"You will see," said Andrew.

Then, the maid got up and left, leaving her cleaning supplies behind. As soon as the maid was out of sight, they quickly crept towards the supplies.

"Do you see how that part of the floor is dirty?" He asked, pointing at a stain on the floor.

"Did you do that?" asked Katelyn

"No, but look at this." He opened the curtain slightly, showing small specks of dirt on the window. "I did that, but that is not all." He got on one knee and lifted the bottom part of the curtain, revealing a purple stain on the wall.

"What is that?" asked Mary.

"Last night, I entered here and squished a grape onto the wall."

"So what do you plan on doing with all these stains? Shall you tell the maids?" asked Katelyn

"No, I plan on cleaning these stains myself."

Katelyn, Mary, and Amelia stood there appalled. "Are you mad, Brother? You cannot do this."

"She is right, Brother," said Amelia, "You know that it is against the law. All Arigogians, especially children, are forbidden to even touch cleaning supplies, for it is against our properness."

"It is just a few stains. If anything, I will be giving the maids a hand."

"The only hand that will be given is Father's when he punishes you," said Katelyn, "Remember, as the children in the royal family, the laws are much stricter upon us. Therefore, we must be obedient."

"Forgive me for my words, but I really do not care about the rules."

"But, Brother you . . ."

"Why does it matter to you, Sister? We will not be ruling Arigog anyway."

"But . . ."

Before Katelyn could begin her sentence, Andrew picked up the floor brush and began to clean the floor. After several minutes, the stain began to disappear.

"It looks easy, and like magic," said Amelia. After a few minutes, the stain was gone. Then he got up and moved on to the window.

"The dirt is not going away. It is just turning into mud. Even the brush is getting filthy."

"Here," said Mary, pushing a bucket of water to Andrew, "Try the water. I have watched the maids.

Whenever the maids add water, the stains would disappear."

Andrew dipped the brush into water and tried again. The mud was instantly reduced to brown water as it dripped down the window.

"Thank you, Mary. This is much easier." Mary, happy to be of good help, stood there blushing.

"All right, Brother," said Amelia, "You have done what you have wanted. You have cleaned the stains. Now we must go."

"Wait. I must clean the last one." Andrew then went back on one knee and began to scrub the grape stain.

Suddenly, they heard footsteps. "Oh, no," said Amelia, "Hurry, Brother, hurry."

"Oh, dear. The grape is stuck. It will not come off."

As Andrew struggled, the footsteps were getting louder and louder. "Hurry," Katelyn whispered, "Someone is getting closer. It might be Agatha, or worse. It might be Mother and Father. Please, Brother, hurry." Andrew tried again, but gave up and dropped the brush into the bucket. Then, they stood together with their backs straight.

To their relief, their favorite brown-haired maid, Daleen, entered the hall. Her great smile and slow walk was soothing to all of them. "Why, hello there, Prince, Princesses, and Mary."

"Hello, Daleen," they all said happily in unison.

"What are you all . . .?"

"Daleen," barked an angry voice, "Who are you talking to?"

"The royal children . . . and friend."

The sound of footsteps filled the air and, to their horror, a skinny, red-haired maid entered the hall. "Hello, children," she said in a nasty tone.

"Hello, Agatha." The children said mournfully in unison.

"And for what reason are you all out here, unattended without guards or maids?"

"We were just walking around, reciting our studies," Mary lied.

"Oh really? Well then, let us hear them. Mary Botin, what is a Vase?"

"A Vase," recited Mary, "is what we treasure. A Vase is what we know and how we live. A Vase is what foretells of our past, present, and days to come. Vases were given to our ancestors, are given to us, and will be given to our children.

We, as Arigogians, people of the land of the red, live by the Vase in happiness and pure properness."

"Good . . . Prince Andrew Asselin!" Andrew jumped. "What happens when you perform actions that are against what is foretold on your Vase?"

"If," Andrew started nervously, "if . . . someone . . . if someone was . . . to go . . . to go against their Vase . . . the skies will strike them."

"Give us a story."

"According to legend . . . a man was foretold to marry an ugly lady, but went against his Vase and married a beautiful lady. That night . . . lightning struck and burned their house, killing the couple . . . therefore, we must always follow what is foretold on our Vases."

"Good. Princess Katelyn Asselin, what happens when you break your Vase?"

"Breaking your Vase," Katelyn recited, "is against nature and is the most inhumane thing you can do. Breaking your Vase damages your future. If you break your Vase, there is a small chance that you can get a new one, but it may foretell horrible things."

"Give us a story."

"According to legend, a brother and sister were foretold to be cooks. They refused and their Vases were broken. The brother broke his Vase on purpose, but the sister broke her Vase by accident. Later that day, the brother went into the crop field. There, lighting struck. It killed him and burned what was to be enough food for a year. The sister received a new Vase, but it foretold that she would now spend the rest of her life as a beggar. Therefore, we must never break our Vases."

"Good. Princess Amelia Asselin."

Amelia stood there terrified. For some reason, she would always be the one who was given the most questions to answer, and whenever she would get one wrong, Agatha would always yell at her.

"For justice to be given, what happens now to those who break their Vase?"

"They . . . they are executed."

"Good. Now, another question. What are Destramechs?"

"Ummm . . . Destramechs . . . are . . . ummm . . . meanies."

"Meanies?" asked Agatha with a loud voice "Is that what they truly are? Meanies?"

"Agatha," Daleen calmly interrupted, "She is young, still learning."

"But, she is the next ruler. She . . . they . . . must know this!"

"They answered almost every question you gave correctly, and yet you anger yourself when the youngest gave one wrong answer. Besides, she is almost right. Destramechs are, in a way, meanies."

Agatha stood there for a few seconds. Then she looked up as a thought came into her head. "I . . . I see what is going on here. I am trying to give discipline and pure order to these children. I am trying to make them as strict and as proper as a human can be. But, you . . . you make it seem as if I am the villain, causing the royal family to favor you. But I see the truth once more and it will not work. You are just trying to sneak your way to becoming Head Maid again!"

This wasn't the first time Agatha mentioned this ever since she became of higher authority than Daleen. For years, Agatha wanted the title of Head Maid, a true honor that she had been fighting for, and a title that Daleen never really cared about.

"Being Head Maid would be a nice honor," said Daleen, "but it is something that you desire. Besides, I'm just happy to be a maid at all."

"Very well. What exactly are you doing here then?"

"I am actually here for Princess Amelia. There is a dress in her room that the Queen wishes for me to finish today."

"Very well."

"Come, Princess. I must finish your dress." Amelia ran and grabbed Daleen's hand. "Oh, and Agatha, I believe that there might be a large spill in the other hallway . . . near the Throne Room." Agatha quickly picked up her dress and ran out of sight.

"Perhaps it is a mess so big that she would be ruined." said Mary.

"Perhaps you should be more careful when you purposely make messes so that way you can clean them yourselves." Everyone, especially Andrew, stood there surprised. "I saw you squish that grape on the wall, Your Highness. I am more than aware that you are trying to clean around here, even when I have told you that it is not a fun thing to do. You all know that I can get you out of trouble from other maids and even Agatha, but if your mother and father were to hear of this, I will not be able to protect you from punishment. Just hide the stains so that way I can get to them when I finish, and please, do not touch another thing. Now, come with me, Princess. Your dress needs to be finished." Holding hands, they walked away, leaving Katelyn, Andrew, and Mary behind.

Time had passed as Amelia grew into the young girl she was expected to be. She, like Madame Leona prophesied, was an obedient child, doing what she was told, making her parents happy. However, as her life began to take form, so did her interest in her Vase. Over the years, Amelia was curious and wondered why a large, polished Vase was in and, no matter what, had to stay in her room on a wooden table. Amelia was trying on a new green dress with Daleen's assistance.

While looking in her mirror, Amelia once again focused her attention on her Vase. Curiosity filled her mind to the point where she could not keep it to herself anymore.

"Daleen?"

"Yes, my dear?"

"Why is my vase in my room?"

"Pardon?" She turned around and looked at what Amelia was talking about. "Ah, you must mean the polished object, my dear."

"Yes. I know it is a vase, but why must there be one in my room?"

"Oh, my dear. It must always be here."

She took Amelia's hand and helped her off her stool. "As you know, a Vase is what we use to tell of our futures, and everyone in the Kingdom has one. Your father, your mother, your siblings . . . . why, even I have a Vase."

"I am aware of that, but how does one get a Vase, Daleen?"

"It is quite easy, Princess. First, a group of people called the Foretellers have visions of a child's entire life. Then, a Vase is sculpted, and everything that they have foreseen is painted onto the Vase and then shined to perfection. Usually, the Vase is foretold and given to the child a month after they are born. However, your Vase was predicted before you were born. Your Vase was completed and given to you when you were one day old."

More curiosity now began to grow in Amelia's heart. It excited her how there were many colorful paintings on the Vase, yet she had no idea what they meant.

"What do they mean?"

"I beg your pardon, my dear?"

"The paintings . . . what do they mean? Can we bring in a Foreteller to interpret for us?"

"Well, lucky for you, my dear, I am quite good at reading Vases. If you wish, I would happily interpret the Vase and read it to you."

"Yes, please. Read it to me."

Daleen then walked Amelia to her Vase.

"Let us see," said Daleen as she carefully placed her finger on the painting of a baby. "You were born as a healthy and very beautiful baby girl, and you have been chosen to take the throne." Then, she moved to the second painting, which was a girl in a pink dress with a halo on her head. "You will live your life happily, being the proper and obedient girl that you must be. You will continue learning to be proper as you are being prepared to be Arigog's future Queen." Daleen then placed her finger on a yellow painting. "Ummmm . . . let us see . . . you will be in a yellow room to celebrate the day of your birth and the day that you are considered a woman. There, a handsome blond-haired man, whom you will know for many years, will ask for your hand in marriage. You will happily say yes, and you two will get married the next day."

Almost instantly, Amelia's smile disappeared. That did not really sound good to her.

"You will happily have many children. As your father steps down, you and your husband will rule Arigog. You will make sure that your children grow properly, as you help bring the lands to true peace. You will soon die of an illness in front of your husband and weeping children. You will have a lovely funeral, then you will be burned, and your ashes will be put into your Vase."

All that Amelia could do was stand there motionless. She had never heard anything more ridiculous in her young life.

"Please tell me that this is not true."

"Pardon, Princess?"

"The Vase. It cannot be true."

"Oh, but it is, Princess. This is what your Vase has foretold for you."

"No. There must be a mistake. This must be a lie."

"No, this is what your life will be."

"Bu . . . but I . . . I do not want this. I do not want to marry. I do not want to be the Queen. I do not want to die and burn."

"I am sorry, but you will, Princess. This is what your Vase says."

"No! I do not believe it! Get rid of it!"

"Pardon me, Princess."

"The Vase! Get rid of it!"

"Forgive me, Princess, but I cannot get rid of it. It is your Vase; it belongs here."

"No! No! No!"

Amelia ran for the door and rushed out of her room.

"Princess . . . Princess! Come back, Princess!"

But Amelia didn't obey. She ran down the stairs, down the hall, and into the throne room. Barona and William were speaking to Madame Leona as she ran in. There next to Barona was Mary, Katelyn, and Andrew. Andrew's face looked red and his pants were wet from what looked like the bucket water.

"Ah, there you are, Daughter," said Barona, "Come here, Daughter. I wish to see your dress."

"Mother, I—"

"Be still, Daughter. I wish to see your dress."

"Father, please. I must tell you something."

"Daughter, listen to your mother and be still."

At last Amelia gave up and obeyed as Barona turned her around.

"The dress is not even finished, but it already looks lovely. Are you almost done Daleen?"

"Yes, my Queen." said Daleen, who came in out of breath.

"My," said William, "it will look great on you when it is finished, Daughter. You have really gotten big. Perhaps we should cease giving you apple tarts for a while."

"Nonsense," said Madame Leona, "She looks fine. She is as beautiful and obedient as her Vase has foretold."

"But I do not wish to have my Vase."

Barona slowly let go of Amelia. "What did you say?"

"I said that I do not wish to have my Vase, Mother."

Barona gave a look of concern, and then smiled. "Daughter, your Vase is important for your life. As the future Queen, what you do may determine the rise and fall of Arigog. Besides, your life is perfect so there should not be a problem."

"But..."

"Daughter, I will not hear another word of this. Now go upstairs and allow Daleen to finish your dress."

Everyone began to walk away as Daleen tried to take Amelia out of the throne room, but Amelia felt as if she could not let her thoughts go unspoken. "But, I do not want my Vase."

Everyone turned around with faces worse than the last. "Wha...what did you say?"

"I do not want it."

"Daughter, obey me and leave."

"But I do not want it!"

"Daughter!"

"I want my vase to be destroyed!"

Everyone was now staring at her with different looks on their faces. As Amelia looked at them, her heart sank. While everyone else was showing pale faces, William and Madame Leona's faces were scarlet.

"Ummm . . . I . . ."

But before Amelia could even say another word, William grabbed her arm so tight that it was hurting. Then he pulled, nearly dragging her out of the throne room with Barona, Daleen, and Madame Leona chasing behind. William then opened her bedroom door, tossed Amelia inside, and slammed the doors closed. Amelia got up and stood there, wondering what she did wrong. Then, William returned with a whip in his hand, grabbed her and struck her with it. Amelia screamed in pain as William struck again, paying no mind to where the whip struck. Then, when he stopped, she was already starting to bleed.

"What are you doing?" called a voice. It was Madame Leona, who was standing inside. "Finish! She must learn her lesson!"

"She is bleeding. I will not."

"You must, my King, or perhaps you would prefer another vision for her, or someone else who is not as merciful to perform this simple task."

William stood there for a moment, then sighed and continued. After several more strikes, he stopped. Amelia's face was covered in tears as scratches opened and her dress was ruined. Without saying another word, William and Leona left while Daleen, Elizabeth, a blonde-haired maid, and Mary came in.

Daleen carefully lifted Amelia up and delicately began removing the torn dress. "It is all right," she whispered, "It is all right. I will make it feel better." Suddenly, Agatha entered, and her eyes widened.

"What happened to her?"

"The princess spoke ill of her Vase and the King had beaten her."

"I will get water and bandages."

"Oh, and bring some apple tarts."

"Daleen, I do not believe that now is the perfect time for apple tar—"

"Please, just bring them."

Agatha quickly ran and returned with a small bowl of water, rags, bandages, and a plate of hot, golden-brown apple tarts. Mary walked toward the bed and watched as the dress was removed, the scratches were cleaned, and Amelia was bandaged.

"It is all right now, Princess," said Daleen as she finished putting a nightgown on her. "See, your friend, Mary, she is here."

Mary walked towards Amelia and carefully gave her a hug. Daleen, feeling sorry for her, delicately did the same.

"I have an idea," she said as she let go. "I say that we all should eat an apple tart. Just one would not hurt. Do you agree, Princess?"

Amelia, still hurting from the whip, simply gave a nod, and Agatha then passed out the apple tarts. Tart in hand,

Amelia sat on the floor sniffling, cuddling in Daleen's loving arms.

Chapter 4:

The Proper Amelia

Nineteen-year-old Amelia was asleep in her room. The sun was not even in the sky yet when her doors were opened, and an older and heavier Daleen entered.

"Princess, it is time to arise."

Amelia crawled herself out of her cold and uncomfortable bed. She immediately got undressed and went to take a bath. After her bath, Daleen gave her a yellow dress to wear, and instantly Amelia frowned.

"I hate that one," she said, "Must I wear that dress?"

"I am afraid so, madam. The Queen requested this dress for you to wear." Without hesitation, Amelia put on the dress.

Daleen then took her hair, combed it, and made it into a bun. After finishing her hair and dabbing an excessive amount of perfume on her, Daleen backed up to look at Amelia.

"There you are, Princess," she said with a smile. Amelia just stared at her with a blank look on her face. Then, Daleen went and opened the doors with Agatha and Elizabeth standing outside. Together, the maids walked behind Amelia down the hall, down the stairs, and into the dining room. The dining room was large with the sun shining in, with butlers, the King, and Queen already inside. The Queen, who was eating her food, stood up and, as every day, walked towards the door. The maids then walked in front of Amelia and curtsied before the Queen.

"Good morning, my Queen." said Daleen.

"Good, morning, Daleen." Barona replied.

"Presenting the Princess for breakfast, my Queen."

"Good."

The maids then walked away as Amelia stepped forward and made a curtsy. "Good morning, Mother." As she said this, she, as every day, pulled herself together and forced herself to make a legitimate, but fake smile.

"Good morning, Daughter. Your breakfast is ready."

"Wonderful." The second Barona turned away to go to the table, Amelia removed her smile and walked towards William, who was still eating.

"Good morning, Father." she said with a curtsey and another fake smile.

"Good morning, Daughter. I believe that you have had good sleep. Is it true?"

"Yes, Father," she lied.

She then went and sat down to eat her breakfast, bland wheat in hot milk with fruit and a glass of water. Amelia, as always, struggled to eat the bland food. When she finished, she gracefully got up and left with Daleen out of the dining room. Together, they walked down the hall to a room full of books and maps. Amelia sat down in a chair as Daleen stood close to the wall.

"Now," she began, "let us recite the basics. What is a Vase?"

"A Vase is what we treasure. A Vase is what we know and how we live. A Vase is what foretells of our past, present, and days to come. Vases were given to our ancestors, are given to us, and will be given to our children. We, as Arigogians, people of the land of the red, live by the Vase in happiness and pure properness."

"Good. Now what happens when you go against your Vase?"

"If someone was to go against their Vase, the skies will strike them. According to legend, a man was foretold to marry an ugly lady, but went against his Vase and married a beautiful lady. That night, lightning struck and burned their house, killing the couple. Therefore, we must always follow what is foretold on our Vases."

"What about breaking your Vase?"

"Breaking your Vase is against nature and is the most inhumane thing you can do. Breaking your Vase damages your future. If you break your Vase, there is a small chance that you can get a new one, but it may foretell horrible things. According to legend, a brother and sister were foretold to be cooks. They refused, and their Vases were broken. The brother broke his Vase on purpose, but the sister broke her Vase by accident. Later that day, the brother went into the crop field. There, lighting struck. It killed him and burned what was to be enough food for a year. The sister received a new Vase, but it foretold that she would now spend the rest of her life as a beggar. Therefore, we must never break our Vases or we will be executed."

"Now, what is Destera?"

"Destera, known as the land of the purple, is a land of evil and improperness. The people, the Destramechs, are as cold as night and are as filthy as vermin. A Destramech is someone who should be hated until they die."

"Good. What are Slavernors?"

"Slavernors are men that hunt for people. They hide in the Revel Forest. Anyone who enters may never come back. Therefore, we must stay in Arigog."

"Good. Now, let me see your etiquette. Show me your curtsy."

Amelia got up and gave Daleen a graceful curtsy.

"Marvelous as always, Princess. And now, I need to see a smile."

Amelia struggled as she made her usual fake smile, making Daleen's smile disappear.

"Why must you keep using that fake smile, Princess? You use it everywhere you go, especially in front of the King and Queen."

"There is not much that makes me happy. Besides, I believe that we both know the aftermath if I was to show my true feelings."

Before Daleen could say another word, Agatha entered with a smile on her face.

"Princess, your friends are here."

"Wonderful," said Amelia as she left the room. All three of them walked down the hall toward the courtyard where there was a garden with flowers in full bloom, showing off their radiant colors while the summer sunshine glowed on their petals. There, a group of girls Amelia's age was sitting quietly in their chairs as they wore happy faces and braided hair, but one of them Amelia recognized immediately as Mary. Her brown hair and simple face made it easy to spot her. As Amelia entered the garden, the ladies stood up and gave their graceful curtsies.

When Amelia sat down, Daleen said, "We will leave you all to yourselves." Then she and Agatha left.

Amelia wanted to beg Daleen to stay or to even ask her to find a way to get her out of here. But she feared that the ladies would tell her mother about her improperness, so she kept her mouth shut.

"Well, this is a lovely day, is it not?" asked one of the ladies. Everyone except Mary and Amelia murmured in agreement. "Casey, your face is shining as bright as a new Vase. Did something happen?" A blonde-haired girl in a blue dress smiled.

"Not yet, but something will happen. I have been foretold to meet my future husband." The girls looked at her

35

in excitement. "According to my Vase, tomorrow is the day that a meadow of yellow flowers will be in bloom. There, I must wait until a man comes and presents me a red flower. That man will be the one that I have been foretold to marry!" All of the ladies clapped with smiles on their faces. Amelia gave her usual fake smile, and Mary looked as if she was going to be sick.

"Oh, speaking of love, I heard that Bartholomew is in the castle, Princess." Everyone then looked at Amelia, eager to hear her response.

"Wonderful."

Suddenly, all of the ladies looked and stood up. Amelia, fearing that it was Mother and Father, turned around and did the same. Instead of the King and Queen, a handsome blond-haired man entered with a prideful smile on his face and with Agatha by his side.

"Presenting Bartholomew Aaron, royal citizen of Arigog, to the Princess." Then, she walked away.

"Lovely day, ladies."

"Hello, Bartholomew." The ladies gave their curtsies as Bartholomew walked straight towards Amelia.

"Good day, Princess."

"Hello . . . Bartholomew."

"Well, aren't you going to curtsy to me?"

"I beg your pardon? You are not of royalty."

"True, but my Aunt, as you know, is Madame Leona. Therefore, I believe that I deserve something. Here, allow me to give it to you." He lowered his head and gave a bow. Amelia reluctantly did the same.

"May I ask as to why you have been invited here?"

"I, in actuality, invited myself, and the royal family simply accepted it. Soon, they will be able to accept me even more once I receive the King's blessing."

"And what makes you think that the blessing will be given to you?"

"Why not? It is on my Vase." He began walking around, looking with his blue eyes at the ladies, who had big smiles of admiration on their faces. "I was foretold to be a handsome baby boy. Through unexplainable circumstances, my parents were pronounced dead and I was to be raised by my Aunt Leona. Through the years, I will become a proper young gentleman. I will then receive the King's blessing and propose to you, Princess. You will then say yes, and we will get married the next day." Amelia tried so hard to keep a smile on her face. "We will have many children as I rise as King of Arigog and finally bring true peace in the land. My wife will sadly die of a disease, and I will unfortunately receive a similar fate. I will have a lovely funeral, be burned, and my ashes will be put into my Vase." Everyone except Amelia applauded.

"My," said one of the ladies, "I am quite surprised that you know your Vase."

"Well, a good man knows best, and since I am the best, I have memorized my Vase entirely. I consider it as a small preparation for the time that I will be spending as King. Well, I must be off. Farewell, ladies and farewell, Princess."

"Farewell."

Bartholomew began to leave. The ladies, eager to be around him, curtsied and followed him, leaving Amelia and Mary to themselves. The second they were gone, Amelia removed her fake smile.

"Mary, let me now say thank you for being one of the only people that I can be myself around and for being nothing like the other ladies." She then looked up. "Oh, how I hate Bartholomew with a passion. I would perhaps rather be a Destramech than to be his wife."

"Bartholomew has some pride, but he is also a great man." They then walked out of the garden and down the hallway.

"I do not understand what everyone sees in him."

"Perhaps you should give him a chance."

"I did. He first came here when I was seven, and I hated him immediately. I later felt bad and tried to give him a second chance the next day. Now, he shows up almost every day, and everyone in the palace treats him as if he is a King, as if he is part of the family. And that shall happen on the day my brother returns with my uncle . . ." Amelia quickly placed her hands over her mouth, hoping that no one else heard her. "I am sorry. I should not have said that."

"It is all right. Speaking of family, can you come with me to the Vase Room to visit Bartholomew's aunt, Madame Leona?"

"You know that I do not enjoy her presence. Besides, my face hurts from forcing a smile."

"Please, Princess. It will only be for a few minutes." Amelia sighed.

"Very well."

"Thank you. You know, Princess, I really did like your brother . . . and I miss him."

"I miss him too, Mary." Amelia walked with Mary, still keeping an eye out for anyone who could have heard her.

It had been two years since her brother, Andrew, disappeared. One rainy night, it was already foretold that he was supposed to meet his future wife in the morning. However, Andrew had already known who the girl was and said that he hated her with all of his heart. He and Father got into a heated argument until Andrew had enough and just left. And she had to be even more careful about mentioning the uncle. Amelia knew that her father had a brother, but according to mother, her uncle ran away, too. No reasons were given as to why he left or why not to mention it, only that Father gets furious if anyone even accidentally mentions his brother. Both were never seen again and their Vases to this day have been left untouched. After a long walk, Amelia and Mary made it to their destination. Standing in front of them were big wooden doors, smaller than, but as old as the doors to the throne room with the design of a Vase carved into the wood. Amelia reached out and knocked. The door opened slightly, and an Elder's voice came out.

"Who is it?"

"It is I, the Princess of Arigog, and friend, Mary." The Elder fully opened the door.

"Of course, Princess and friend. How may we serve you two?"

"We wish to see Madame Leona."

"Unfortunately, Madame Leona is very busy. She is assisting a new Foreteller who claims to have had his first visions, and they are now starting on a Vase. Perhaps another ti—"

"Elder," said a voice, "Did you say that the princess is at the door?"

"Yes, Madame."

The Elder left and was replaced with an older Madame Leona. "Hello, Princess."

"Hello, Madame Leona." Amelia said with a curtsy and a fake smile.

"It is good to see you. You know, some good events that have been foretold on your Vase are about to come to pass."

"Of course. Thank you, Madame Leona."

"So, to what do I owe the pleasure?"

"My friend, Mary, wishes to speak to you."

Leona's eyes slowly moved from Amelia to Mary. "Yes?"

"I wish to ask something . . . something about my Vase."

"Yes, go on."

"Are . . . are you sure that all that my Vase says is what it will be?"

"Why, yes."

"Are . . . are you sure that there is nothing else?"

"My child, your Vase, like everyone else's, is made with extreme care, especially with its foretellings. Are you telling me that you question the ways of the Vases?"

"No."

"Then what in heaven's name would you want changed?"

"Love."

"Pardon?"

"Madame Leona . . . you foretold that I will live my life alone. No husband . . . no children . . . nothing. Are you sure that this is correct? Is there a way that we could . . . make a new one?"

"I understand. Unfortunately, I cannot. The visions that were given were quite precise. If we were to make a new one, they may come with some . . . unlikable fortunes. Something of which I am certain that you do not want."

"Of course not, Madame."

"Good. Now, if you will excuse me, I must help with the beginnings of a new Vase. Farewell." And with that, she closed the door.

"Well," said Mary as they left, "at least we have tried. Thank you for coming. I become quite nervous around her."

"It is all right."

They then spent the rest of the time walking down the halls, talking about their Vases and what they desire.

"So, how many children do you want, Princess?"

"To be honest, none."

"How many children did your Vase foretell?"

"Many, I believe. We could look at my Vase to be sure." They went upstairs, into Amelia's room, and walked to her dresser, where stood her Vase. "I was correct. I was foretold to have many children. I remember when it was foretold to me a while ago. It will happen after I am married . . . after my birthday."

"Princess," Mary said softly, "I know that you do not enjoy speaking of it, but your birthday is in several days." Amelia stared at the yellow painting of the couple and the blue painting of the wedding. "Princess . . . when was the last time you read your Vase?"

43

"Mary," Amelia said, now feeling irritated, "You and I both know that I have not read my Vase since . . . well . . . you know." Amelia walked over and sat on her bed. Mary slowly went over and sat next to her.

"I . . . I am sorry, Princess."

"It is . . . it is all right."

"Do you . . . do you still have . . . the scars?"

"Mary, of course I do." Amelia pulled her sleeve, revealing deep, straight scars on her back and neck.

It had been fourteen years since Amelia was beaten by her father, and it had left both physical and mental scars on her.

"Who would have thought that those marks would never go away? And all because you spoke ill of your Vase."

"I remember things were happier when we were little. But ever since he had beaten me, nothing has been, nor do I believe will ever be the same."

Before they could say anything else, Elizabeth entered. "Dinner is ready, Princess."

"I believe that I should return home now," said Mary. The three them walked down the stairs and down the hall. Mary and Amelia hugged and they went their separate ways, with Mary leaving the palace and Amelia and

Elizabeth heading to the dining room. There, the King and Queen were already eating. Amelia sat down and looked at her meal, cooked cattle with fruit.

"Daughter," said Barona, "I noticed that Bartholomew was in the palace. Did he see you?"

"Yes, Mother."

"Good. You know, Daughter, he has shown up here for a very long time. Perhaps in a way, this is his home. After all, he was only raised by his aunt."

Perhaps he has grown a little bored of his life and continues to come and ruin mine. Amelia thought, but she knew that she couldn't say those words.

"Barona," said William, "I have been wondering. Have you heard from Katelyn lately?"

"Yes, indeed I have. In fact, she sent me a letter today. As foretold in her Vase, she and her husband have had their second child now. Yet, she has told me that she is sad and how things have not been the same ever since . . . our son left . . . performed the same actions as his un – "

"*Don't* mention him," barked William. Barona quickly stopped talking, and the rest of dinner was in silence. After dinner, Amelia and Daleen went upstairs to the bedroom. Amelia got into her nightgown and Daleen prepared her bed. Instead of getting in the bed, Amelia stood there and stared at her Vase.

"Daleen?"

"Yes, Princess?"

"My birthday is getting nearer, is it not?"

"Yes it is, Princess."

"And I will be a woman and of marrying age?"

"This is true, Princess." Amelia then stood there in silence, staring at the object that told of her life. "I know that it does not make you happy, but I know what will." Amelia turned around as Daleen stood in front of her, holding an apple tart in a towel. "I had managed to sneak one for you, Princess."

"Thank you." Amelia took and ate the tart.

"Well, I will leave you to yourself. Goodnight, Princess."

"Goodnight, Daleen."

Daleen left and closed the door as Amelia blew out the candle next to her bed and went to sleep.

Chapter 5:

Preparations

Mary was right. As days went by, Amelia began to notice a few odd things going on. For some reason, the maids were becoming busy, her mother and father were always talking in private, and she was even fitted for a dress. Amelia had just finished her lunch one day and proceeded to head up to her room. As she was walking, she noticed a wall. There was a large door with a pillar on each side, which she easily recognized as the ballroom entrance.

To Amelia's curiosity, the door was opened to the room, in which the decorations had been left unfinished. The room had many large pillars draped with silky yellow curtains, and her parents were in the middle of the room in a deep conversation. Amelia knew that she couldn't just sneak up on them, but her desire to know what they were saying was increasing. So with great caution, she began to creep into the room. She tiptoed carefully, nearly slipping as she made sure her parents' backs were turned. After what felt like several minutes, she was able to hide behind one of the pillars, being completely incognito from view. Then, she kept herself quiet as she heard what they were saying.

"I am truly excited," said Barona, "do you think she will be happy?"

"Of course," William replied. He walked a few steps and then turned around with a smile on his face. "It is not every day a girl gets to celebrate the day she becomes a woman. I am sure that by the time we are done, she will be amazed by the celebration . . . and the surprise."

"Even though it is on her Vase, we are not fully sure if he would accept it, my King. We have not even asked him yet."

"Why would he not? Having the King's blessing is something men would kill and die for. It is an extraordinary honor. I would be quite upset if it is declined, but I do not see as to why he would."

Suddenly, the sound of footsteps went into Amelia's ears. She was able to poke her head out just a little bit as Daleen entered the room out of breath.

"Why hello, Daleen," said Barona, "I suppose that you have news for us."

"Yes, my Queen," Daleen replied, panting and giving a curtsy. "I was able to do as you requested and summoned all of the maids and servants. They are waiting outside the doors as we speak."

"Good."

"Also, Bartholomew has received Your Majesty's invitation and is now waiting outside the doors as well."

"Ah, yes," William replied abruptly. "Send him in first."

"Yes, Your Majesty." Daleen replied with another curtsy and then scurried out of the ballroom. Concerned, Amelia wanted to get Daleen's attention, but she kept quiet and hid.

Oh, dear, Amelia thought. *Will they really give it to Bartholomew, of all people?*

A few minutes later, Daleen returned with Bartholomew. He entered with his head held high and a smile of pride on his face, which made Amelia want to throw up. When they were at a close distance to the King and Queen, Daleen announced, "Presenting Bartholomew Aaron, son of the wealthy Aaron family, citizens of Arigog, to the royal King and Queen."

"Thank you, Daleen," said Barona, "Now if you may, please wait outside. We wish to be alone for a moment. We will summon you when we are finished."

Then, Daleen scurried out of the room again, closing the doors behind her.

"Ah, Bartholomew. It is good to see you," said William.

"It is truly good to be here, my King and Queen," Bartholomew replied as he took a slow and graceful bow. "To what do I owe the pleasure?"

"As you know," William slowly began to walk, "my daughter's very special day will be here soon. The princess will be of marrying age in just a few days."

"Really? I did not know that."

"Yes, and according to her Vase, she will happily say yes to a man who will propose to her on that night and will get married the next day. Now, I have known you for a few years, Bartholomew, and so has my daughter. You also are exactly as the Vase described. You come here almost every day, as if this is your home. I believe it is time to make a good change around here. How would you like to be my son-in-law, husband to the princess?"

"I am not fully understanding, my King. Are you giving me your blessing?"

"Yes. If you are willing to accept the blessing I am offering, you will have my daughter and will be able to rule as King of Arigog."

Bartholomew lowered his head, as if he was pondering about the opportunity given to him. Amelia had already known his answer, considering he was thinking about it for quite too long and the fact that he had been bragging about being the future king for years. Then, he lifted his head even higher, as if pride was pouring out of him. "Very well. I will happily accept your blessing and marry the princess."

"Splendid!" William replied, giving Bartholomew a gargantuan hug. Amelia almost fainted. She could not believe what had just happened. "Hazaaa! Arigog will now have a new king! Oh, but do not tell her."

"Of course, Your Majesty. I will not tell a word of this to her. Well then, if you would please excuse me, I must prepare myself for this tremendous event."

"Wait, Bartholomew. I need to come with you. There are a few important things that must be done for you in preparation of this celebration."

Very well. In that case, farewell, my Queen."

"Farewell, Bartholomew." Barona replied

And with that, Bartholomew took a final bow and began to walk out of the ballroom. William then went and began walking next to him with his arm on his shoulder.

I . . . I do not believe this, Amelia thought. *I have not even been proposed to, and yet my father it is already treating him like a son.*

As soon as they had walked out, Daleen walked in. "Shall I bring them in, my Queen?"

"Yes," Barona replied with a smile. Daleen curtsied and went to open the doors. The maids and servants quickly entered the room and stood in two rows. On the row to the Queen's left were the servants and on her right were the maids, all standing tall and waiting for orders. "As you all happily know," started Barona as she began to walk, "the princess will become a woman in a few days, and to celebrate this joyous occasion, a party is to be held. I would also like to announce that as of a few minutes ago, Bartholomew has received the royal blessing and will ask the princess for her hand in marriage." The servants and maids immediately started talking. The servants made short conversation while the maids giggled and jumped with joy. Then, they quickly got themselves together and stood silently. "Now," Barona continued, "who is in charge of the celebration?" A young, tall servant stepped forward and bowed.

"That would be me, Your Majesty."

"Has everything been prepared?"

"Yes, Your Majesty."

"Is my daughter's dress completed?"

"Almost, Your Majesty"

"Have the decorations, invitations, and ideas for the dinner been completed?"

"Yes, Your Majesty. All has been planned out and scheduled. We will have everything set out. Then, we will seat the guests, then you and the King, and then the princess. After that, the celebration will commence with the King saying a few words. Then, there will be dancing, food, and presents. And finally, a thank you from the King and the party ceases."

"Perfect," said Barona, "However, I wish to make a few changes. First, before the presents, Bartholomew must go and propose to the princess. Also, the King wishes for her Vase to be placed on a pedestal in the middle of the room."

The servant had an upset expression on his face, as did many other servants and maids. Then, he erased the look and said, "Not a problem, Your Majesty."

"Good. That is all." And with that, all of the maids and servants bowed and left the room, leaving Barona to herself as she walked toward the nearby window. She was probably imagining that happy smile Amelia is somehow supposed to have when she sees the surprise and when Bartholomew proposes to her. She then turned around and stood surprised. Amelia looked toward the direction her mother was facing. Daleen was still in the room, standing there with a worried appearance on her face, as if a small child who has knowingly done wrong. "Is something the matter, Daleen?" Daleen quickly walked to Barona and stopped a few feet from her.

"If I may ask, why does the King wish to have her Vase for all to see when it is meant to stay in her room?"

"I agree. It does sound ridiculous, but the King thinks that it would be a great thing to add in the celebration." She finished answering the question, expecting Daleen to curtsey to her and leave. Instead, Daleen still stood there with the same face. "Anything else wrong, Daleen?"

"Yes," Daleen replied, "I have something…I should have told you a long…time…ago about the princess, Your Majesty."

"What?" Amelia whispered to herself.

"Yes, go on," her mother replied.

Daleen took another step closer. "As of course you know, my Queen, I am not Head Maid of the palace, but I am the princess's nurse. I have been there with her since she was born, and there is something you must know about her."

"Yes?"

Daleen stepped forward again. "I have been with her for years and she . . . she talks to me. She has told me things. Many things that you would never think that she would think or say."

"Like what, exactly?"

"She said that sometimes she would always see a girl walking or playing with her friends. She told me that sometimes she wishes that she was that girl, to have the childhood like hers. She sometimes said that she wished that her childhood was better than the one that she had." Daleen finished and held her breath. Although it was not much for anyone to get angry about, Amelia worried that Daleen might have already said too much and did the same.

"Yes, go on," Barona replied in a calm voice.

"She had also said that she never liked that Bartholomew. She considers him a selfish and spoiled man with his heart full of pride. She said that she would rather die than marry him. I . . . I too agree with this. I was the maid, years ago, who jumped for joy when her Vase was interpreted at the celebration of her birth, but now I would rather her not be married if it means that she gets to be happy."

Barona was bewildered. "What? That sounds absurd. Why would she not like him? I think he is perfect for her. After all, her Vase says that he is the one. Does she read her Vase?"

Daleen appeared more terrified than ever. "She . . . she does not."

"Do not tell her," Amelia breathed. "Do not tell her."

Daleen took another step forward. "A . . . a few years ago, when she was a little girl, she was curious about the Vase that was in her room and questioned the paintings on them. I am good at interpreting Vases, and I told her exactly what each of the paintings meant. She…she then got upset, really upset. That is why she came to the throne room that day, saying that she did not want her Vase. She has not looked at her Vase since and to this day loathes each and every day, knowing that her time of marrying age is getting closer."

"But the Vase says that she will be happy! I really do not understand."

Daleen attempted to speak, hesitated, and then finally spoke, "She . . . she . . . she hates her life. She thinks that she is burdened with her birth as the future Queen! She hates the fact that the men only want her for her beauty and the throne."

"Do not say it," Amelia repeated. "Do not say it."

"And...and...and she hates her Vase! She hates the fact that her whole life was told on it. She has told me that she has the dream to...to..."

"To what?" Barona asked with her full attention.

"She...she... she wants to destroy it! She told me that she dreams that one day, she will have the courage to go and destroy her own Vase!!"

"Enough!" Barona shouted. "I have heard enough! I refuse to hear any more of these lies!"

"But . . . but Your Majesty. They are not lies. This is from her heart. She truly means every word."

"I do not believe this!"

"I swear on my own life that this is the truth."

Barona began to calm down as tears started to flow from Daleen's eyes. Even Amelia began to cry. She had never seen her mother so angry, and she had never seen Daleen so upset.

"Very well. I will just have to hear it from her whether or not she says yes to Bartholomew, but I doubt she will say no. Until then . . . ," she pointed her finger straight at Daleen, "You will not breathe a word of this to anyone, especially to the King."

"Bu…but . . ."

"You should be grateful that being silent of this is your punishment. If the King was here, he would personally cut your throat." Daleen quickly grabbed her neck with both hands. "Now, do not tell anyone this, especially at the celebration. If I hear you speak of this, I will make sure that you are banished from Arigog forever! Have I made myself clear?"

"I . . . I . . . y-yes, Your Majesty." And with that, Daleen curtsied and left the room, feeling ashamed and disgraced.

As every day was getting closer to her birthday, Amelia began noticing things even more. The maids were now spending more time in the kitchen and everywhere else than ever, and the ladies, and even Bartholomew, had not come to the castle. But she also saw other things. Not just yellow decorations, but white decorations and flowers, had been showing up everywhere she looked. One time as Amelia walked down the hall, a group of maids were huddling in a room. As Amelia got closer, one of the maids looked up quickly.

"Oh, dear. Hello, Princess. I apologize, but we cannot allow you in." The maid ran towards the door, and as she was closing it, Amelia got a short glance at what looked like a white lacy dress.

On the night before her birthday, Daleen was preparing the bed and Amelia sat in her nightgown. She could not believe what was happening. Her birthday was the next day, and everyone was expecting her to say yes to a wedding that had already been prepared for long before the proposal.

"Your bed is ready, Princess."

"Thank you, Daleen."

"I also have something special for you." Amelia turned around and stood up, amazed. Instead of the usual one, Daleen was holding a whole plate of hot apple tarts.

"Th-thank you, Daleen . . . but I am afraid that I do not wish to have any tonight." Daleen's smile disappeared into a disappointed frown.

"Oh, that is all right, Princess. It was just a simple surprise."

Amelia could not hold in her thoughts any longer. She needed to tell Daleen how she felt and she needed to do it now. "Was it as much of a surprise as the party . . .," she said, ". . . or the blessing given to Bartholomew for the next day's wedding?" Daleen's eyes widened as she lowered the plate onto the bed.

"How . . . how did you . . ."

"I snuck into the ballroom that day. I saw and heard everything. I saw the blessing being given to Bartholomew, I saw the maids and servants, and I even saw you." Daleen's face turned white, as if a big secret had just revealed itself. "You told my mother everything . . . I gave you the truths of my heart . . . and you told her *everything*! Why? Why would you do that?"

"To . . . to help you, Princess. I spent too many years watching you suffer and letting it go unspoken. I know that you are miserable now, but I cannot even imagine what your life will be like if this proposal goes forth. I thought that maybe if I was to say something, perhaps there would be some form of change."

"Well, I am happy that you have tried, but it did not work. Instead, you are threatened with exile and everything still goes on as normal." She then sat down and began to cry. "Why must I live this life?" She sobbed. "Never allowed to make my own decisions, only forced to live according to what was told on a stupid piece of clay! I wish that I could destroy my Vase!" Amelia cried, and then felt Daleen hugging her and drying her tears.

"Princess, please do not cry, Princess. Shhhh . . . please do not cry."

"No! I do not even care about what happens to me anymore! I do not care if lightning kills me! Just let me break it and die!"

After several minutes of hugging and tear drying, Amelia began to calm down. It really felt good that when she felt sad or miserable, Daleen would become motherly and give her comfort and strength when she needed it. When Daleen felt Amelia was not going to cry again, she went and picked up the plate of now warm apple tarts. "Princess?"

"Yes, Daleen?"

"Is it all right if I ask you something?"

Amelia sat up. "Sure. What is it?"

Daleen lifted the plate. "You are the Princess of Arigog. Other than what is foretold on your Vase, there are only a few things that the people of Arigog know about you. But, if there is one thing we know about you, it is this: you love apple tarts. Ever since I gave you your first one when you were four, you would eat them every day. But, for the first time ever, a whole plate of tarts has been presented to you, and you have not even touched one. Why is that?"

"Because I am not hungry..."

"Wrong!"

Amelia sat there baffled. "Wait. I take that back, Princess. That is correct, but that is not the answer that I truly was looking for. It is because you do not want one." Amelia stared at her confused.

"I do not understand what you are trying to make out of all of this."

Daleen began to walk around with the plate in hand. "Like how you have chosen whether or not you would want an apple tart, you as a living being can choose as to whether or not you will say yes to Bartholomew's proposal. I believe that everyone has a choice, both good and bad. It may not be what others want or say it should be, but it is your choice.

Hearts will break, but they will still beat. People will be shocked, but in the end, life will go on."

"Bu . . . but . . . my father . . . he . . . he would . . ."

"Tonight is the last night that he, as your father, controls you. Once the sun rises tomorrow, you will be a woman. You will be out of your father's clutches and away from his hand and whip."

Amelia sat there completely shocked. "What about the legend? What if lighting strikes me?"

"Your . . . uncle and brother went against their Vases. When they left, it broke the King and Queen's hearts, yet their hearts still beat and no one has told any new stories of men being struck by lightning. I am sure that if they can do it, you can too."

All that Amelia could do was smile. "Thank you, Daleen, for your words."

"You are most welcome, Princess. Goodnight." Daleen was about to head for the door.

"Daleen, wait." Daleen quickly turned around.

"Yes, Princess?"

"I . . . I want you to eat the apple tarts with me." Both of them smiled as Daleen sat down, and together they both ate the apple tarts.

Chapter 6:

The Birthday

At long last, Amelia's twentieth birthday arrived. She was thinking about what Daleen said so much that she could barely sleep. Amelia came into the dining room looking down at the floor and had a blank look on her face. Her brown hair was braided, and she was in a beautiful blue dress as she was accompanied by Daleen and another maid. Barona, who was eating with William, quickly got to her feet and went to Amelia.

"Good morning, Daughter! Today is truly your special day!" Amelia slowly looked up.

"Good morning, Mother."

"Are you excited?"

"Yes." Amelia then quickly made a fake smile.

As she went to her seat to eat, she overheard her mother speaking to Daleen, who still looked worried. "See, I know she looks truly happy now, but she will be even happier tonight, you shall see." Barona then went to join her family.

Hours quickly passed as the time for the celebration was getting closer. The ladies who accompanied Amelia in the garden only talked about the birthday. Mary, however, gave a look as if she was reading Amelia's soul and could see the true feelings of her life-long friend. After the ladies left, Amelia was accompanied into her room. When the doors were closed, Daleen went into the closet and pulled something out. It was a long red dress with a yellow design on it.

"I had just finished it a few days ago. It is for your . . . dinner." Amelia had already known what Daleen actually meant, but she put on the dress without hesitation. Of all the years Amelia had to try on dresses, this was probably the most uncomfortable dress she had ever had to wear.

"It is tight."

"Forgive me, Princess, but this is how the Queen wants it." As Daleen finished putting the dress on, Amelia stared into the mirror. This moment reminded her of when she was six, wearing the green dress. She looked, and instead of seeing what had brought her curiosity years ago, her Vase was gone, leaving nothing but an empty dresser. After getting changed, Amelia walked down into the dining room.

"Wait," cried Agatha, who was acting as if she was expecting her to come here. "Due to the request of the King and Queen, dinner will be served in the ballroom." And with that, she ran upstairs. Amelia then kept going and walked toward the closed ballroom doors. She could hear a person shouting.

"Presenting the Princess for her twentieth birthday!" After a moment, the doors opened, and Amelia stepped inside. Just like it said on the Vase, the room had yellow decorations. At the far end of the room, a long table was placed, and several round tables were placed in front of it. Everyone in the room applauded as Barona went to Amelia.

"Is this not a wonderful surprise?" Amelia quickly tried to come up with the right words.

"Ummm…. y...yes." Amelia then tried to do her fake smile. She did this for several seconds and finally gave up, keeping a blank look on her face. Barona quickly led Amelia to her seat at the long table. She stared at all of the people that were present. There was Mary, sitting with her family, and Katelyn was sitting with her husband. All of the ladies that Amelia had been around in the garden were all sitting together. The Elders and Madame Leona were sitting at the long table with William, while Bartholomew was showing off his smile as he was sitting at a table with a few other people. Then, she looked, and there, standing in the middle of the room protected by guards, was her Vase on top of a white pedestal. Her heart sank. Tonight was the moment that she had been forced to be prepared for. In a little while, Bartholomew is going to expect her to be his bride. Her face began to turn pale as she and Barona went to their seats. As Amelia sat down, it felt as if her face was trying to think of an acceptable facial expression. But after few minutes of trying, she gave up and, for the first time in years, decided to frown.

Then, William stood up. "It is with great honor that I celebrate with you today the birth of the princess, who is now a woman. And now, let this celebration begin."

The second he said that, a group of dancers presented themselves in front of the table and performed, but Amelia was too shocked to even realize that there were people performing at all. When the dancers left, the servants came in, holding large plates of hot, delicious food. Amelia spent most of the meal time staring at her Vase, too upset to even taste the food given to her. Sometimes, she would pick up a forkful, but just when the fork was about to reach her lips, she would change her mind and place it back down. What was she going to do? Should she accept his proposal so her mother and father could be happy? Should she listen to Daleen and say no? What if the legend is true and lightning does strike her? What will happen to Daleen? To Arigog? To her?

When the plates were removed, William stood up and said, "And now, if the princess would be so kind as to go near her Vase. Bartholomew has a very special surprise for you."

Amelia came back to focus when she heard William's request. This was it. This was the great milestone that everyone was expecting to come into place. Amelia hesitated and then obeyed her father. She got up and slowly made her way to her Vase, with Bartholomew right behind her. When they both got to the Vase, the guards walked away, and all went quiet as Bartholomew spoke.

"As you all know, I have known the princess for a very long time as a friend, but tonight, I wish to no longer be her friend. I now wish to be something more." He grabbed Amelia's hand, got on one knee, and said, "How would you like to be Amelia Aaron, future Queen of Arigog?"

There was cheering and shouting as Amelia looked around. "Now, say yes," Barona mouthed. "Say yes. Say yes." Amelia looked at everyone and then down at Bartholomew, who was smiling even brighter tonight. If what Daleen said was true, then tonight will be the time she can make her own decision.

She lifted her head high, opened her mouth, and said, "No."

The silence returned, but this time a bit quieter. Amelia stood there, expecting a large flash of lighting to come through the ceiling and kill her. She felt no pain and instead looked around. Barona's smile began to disappear, and William's face began to turn pink. Even Madame Leona showed a look of great concern.

Bartholomew, a little confused, asked, "What did you say, my dear?"

"No."

"But..."

"No, I am not going to marry you."

He then stood up, turning pink as well. This was exactly the answer that he was not at all expecting. "I . . . I do not understand. I am exactly as your Vase described. My Vase had this date perfectly prophesied. I even received the royal blessing."

"Yes, but that does not mean I am not allowed to say no."

"But, I do not understand?" Barona said, now standing up and walking towards them. "Your life is perfect. You were born beautiful, you are in line for the throne, you are even proposed to by a man that you have known for years and you say 'no'?"

"I never liked Bartholomew. If you ask me, he is a prideful, selfish, and spoiled boy!"

Barona looked straight at Daleen, who simply responded with a smirk and a nod. It really felt good for Amelia, that she and Daleen both proved her mother wrong.

"But . . . this is not the ways of my daughter. I know my daughter, my real daughter. She—"

"You do *not* know me!" Amelia almost laughed at that statement. "You never knew *anything* about the real me! This is the first time you have come to try to know me, and it is when I have decided for myself that I am going to do things differently than what a Vase says."

"But of course I know you; I am your mother. I have been there for you."

"No, you have *not*! Where were you when I found out what my Vase meant? Where were you when I was expressing my feelings? Where were you when I was being whipped by my own father?"

"But," Barona began "I know you love your foretold life..."

"How *dare* you try to tell me what I do and do not like! I do not love it. I *hate* it!" Amelia closed her eyes as hatred began to consume her "I hate my birth. I hate this life. And . . . and . . . and I hate this stupid vase!"

At that second, many things began to happen at once. Amelia began to get out of control as Barona tried to calm her down. Guards, servants, and maids began to come from all sides. Bartholomew was stepping backward while William was beginning to yell. As Amelia moved, she felt something cold touch her fingertips. She felt a smooth, but icy surface on her hands. She then took all of the rage that was in her mind and placed it into her arms. She pushed the object until she could no longer feel the surface on her fingers.

CRASH!

The room felt dead. It was as if every form of sound was immediately silenced. Amelia, now too scared to know what just happened, slowly opened her eyes. Everyone stood where they were, as if frozen solid. She looked around as every smile was replaced with horrified faces. Barona stood completely terrified, and William, whose face was just about to become scarlet, turned white as a ghost. Even Bartholomew looked pale, as if every ounce of his pride had drowned in fear. A few people were looking at her, but most of them were staring down at the floor. Amelia slowly looked down too, and her eyes widened. She did it. Her dream had finally come true; there, on the floor next to the fallen pedestal, was her Vase, shattered in many pieces.

Chapter 7:

Change of Fate

What did you do? Amelia thought, as she stared at her now broken Vase. *What did you do? What . . . did . . . you . . . do?* The anger that she had was consumed by fear of what was to happen next. Her Vase was the very thing that represented her life. Now, it lay on the floor, broken and out for all eyes to see. She began to realize that she needed to leave . . . now. Before she was able to notice, she was stepping away. *You have got to get out of here. You need to get out of here!* She looked around to find the exit, but it was almost as if the doors had disappeared. While looking for the door, her eyes kept finding the Vase, her guest, and her family. *The Vase is gone, Amelia. It is gone. There is nothing you can do here. You must get out of here . . . now! Oh, my goodness, where is that door?* After what felt like an hour, she at last found the door. As the room began to look like a long maze, she walked past the guests, through the doors and out of the ballroom.

She kept a calm pace passing the guards as she walked down the hall and towards the stairs. Then, when she felt absolutely certain that no one was following her, she picked up her dress, broke into a run and didn't stop until she was at her bedroom door. She flung the door opened to find Agatha inside, stuffing something into the closets that Amelia knew was supposed to be her wedding dress. Agatha, whose head was lowered at the moment, looked up surprised, as if she was caught sneaking.

"Oh, hello, Princess," she responded. "Forgive me; I was just about to come to your celebration as soon as I . . . w-what is wrong?" Amelia closed her door and sat on the bed, feeling empty, cold, and hopeless. "My lady, you look pale. What has happened? My dear, can you hear me?"

"Agatha," Amelia started, "Go and stand outside the door. Unless a maid requests entrance, please make sure that no one enters this room."

Agatha gave a look of confusion and fear. Nevertheless, she curtsied and headed for the door. But before Agatha reached for the handle, the door opened and, to Amelia's relief, Mary entered.

"My dear Mary," Agatha said, "What is going on? You look as pale as the princess."

"Pr-princess . . ."

"Yes. What about her?"

"S-she . . . she . . ." But Mary couldn't even finish the sentence. All that she could do was slightly lift her finger and point to Amelia.

"My dear, what did you do?" Agatha asked as she ran to the bed.

Amelia looked up, feeling as if she was about to cry. She had never felt so scared in her life. "I . . . I broke my Vase."

"Y-you what?"

"My Vase. I broke my Vase."

"Impossible. Your Vase is downstairs, protected by our most trusted guards. How can it be broken?" Amelia then told her about what happened. When she had finished, the room was silent. "I . . . I . . . I do not believe this!" Mary stared at Agatha in disbelief. "Do not pretend as if you are surprised!" She pointed her finger at Amelia in deep anger. "Madame Leona prophesied that she was to be perfect. When she was a child, she said that she hated and threatened to destroy her Vase. Oh, but the King ended that quickly, and she became the proper girl that she was supposed to be. Now is the night that she was to be proposed to and suddenly she says no *and* claims that she has destroyed her Vase? This I do not believe! Not a single bit..."

"I am afraid this is the truth," interrupted a gentle voice. Daleen stood at the door, and Elizabeth was at her side, holding a small basket with a long piece of cloth covering it. Daleen's face was still pale, but rosy as she went straight to Amelia, who stood up and hugged her.

"Elizabeth," Agatha began, still looking at Amelia, "Is it true? The Vase. It is it really broken?"

"Yes," Elizabeth answered, stepping into the room and closing the door. "Amelia pushed her Vase off of the pedestal. It fell, and the painting of her proposal was the first to be destroyed. Because that part of it was the most damaged, the Vase is completely beyond repair. Here, see for yourselves." Elizabeth removed the cloth off the basket, revealing the pieces of Amelia's Vase. Silence filled the room as Agatha took the basket from Elizabeth's hands and placed the pieces onto the table. Then, she slowly took two large pieces and put them together, showing the painting of a baby.

"We are lucky." Elizabeth said, breaking the silence, "The Vase could have hurt the princess. At least we know that she is safe. I—"

"Safe?" Daleen shouted, "Are you mad? The Princess is far from safe! She has broken the biggest law in the book. For she has intentionally broken her Vase in the presence of every person of high royal authority, including the King himself. As far as I know, she is in great danger. When we left the ballroom, everyone was still in shock. Oh, but once they come to their senses, the princess will be taken to be executed!"

"WHAT?" Mary shouted. "*Execute* her? This does not make sense."

"I am afraid that it is the law."

"But . . . but . . . she is a princess . . . the next line to the throne! They can *not* just execute her!"

"They *can* and probably *will*! She is an adult now. She has been taken from the rules of her father and into the laws of the land. It does not matter how high of royalty a person is. If they are to break a rule, they will be punished to the fullest extent of the law." Daleen then faced Amelia so that way their eyes met. "Princess, listen to me. As of now, you are in grave danger. You can no longer call this place your home. You must leave Arigog."

"What?" Amelia began, "For how long?"

"I do not know. But one thing is for sure. You must leave tonight." Daleen stared at the maids. "Elizabeth! I need you to go into the kitchen, grab as much food as you can carry, and bring it here. Then, I need you to go into my room. Under my bed, there should be a small bag and cloak. Bring it here immediately." Elizabeth looked confused. "Go, Elizabeth!" Elizabeth ran out of the room. "Mary, please go with her." Mary nodded and ran out of the room.

"What are you doing?" Agatha demanded. "You cannot give orders."

"Forgive me, but if you may not be able to tell, this is urgent."

"But I am the one who will be Head Maid. The other maids and I are above you. I give commands, not you. I..."

"Can you not see that this is a problem that is life-threatening?"

"But..."

"This is a matter beyond your understanding, Agatha." Daleen then returned her attention to Amelia. "Once

Elizabeth and Mary return, you must leave the palace. You will be safe once you head into the Revel Forest."

"The Revel Forest?" Agatha asked. "Absolutely not! It is dangerous for a princess to go there."

"I do not believe she has any other choice." Before Agatha could say another word, Elizabeth and Mary entered, out of breath and arms full of fruits, small jugs, and meats. Mary was also holding in one hand a small, worn out brown bag with a hole on the front, and Elizabeth was holding a long old brown cloak. "Ugh! I never did like this bag. I used it when I first came here, and for some reason I wanted to keep it. Now I am glad that I did."

Mary was breathing the hardest as she tried to speak. "We (*gasp*) got as much as (*gasp*) our arms could carry (*gasp*). We were almost caught (*gasp*). Several guests (*gasp*) might have seen us."

"Quickly, place the food into the bag." They opened the bag as instructed and placed the stuff inside. Meanwhile, Daleen took the cloak and placed it on Amelia. "We must go to the forest without being seen. I..."

"I wish to go alone."

"What?" Both Daleen and Agatha responded.

"Oh, perfect," Agatha said in despair. "First, the next in line to the throne breaks her Vase. Now, she wishes to travel alone. What shall happen next?"

"What do you mean, my dear?" Daleen asked as Agatha began to lecture to herself.

"I am going alone, Daleen. You have taught me all that I would need. You have shown me so much, of which I am truly grateful. Besides, if we get caught, you will share my burdens, and I will never be able to forgive myself."

"What I have taught you is what is needed as the future Arigogian Queen. What is needed outside these walls is very different."

"You must not be serious," said Mary. "I am sure that there is something that we have been taught that will be helpful. I mean, Princess, have you ever been inside the forest?"

"Mary, I have never been outside of this castle. I do not even know what dirt or grass feels like."

"What about the garden?"

"In the garden, I was never allowed to touch anything, only to sit in the chair and talk to the other ladies that were with us."

"Please . . . just let us come with you. Just so that way we will know that you left safely."

"Well, . . . I . . . all right."

And with that, Elizabeth grabbed the bag with Mary by her side. Daleen, feeling protective, held onto Amelia as they headed for the door. Agatha, who now realized that no one was listening to her, ran and stood in front of them, blocking the exit.

"Wait just a moment. Where do you all think you shall be going? The princess must not leave the palace. It is against the law."

"We must go." Daleen said softly.

"No! I will not allow it. I—"

"Listen here, you grouchy old woman!" Mary shouted, stepping in front of Agatha. "You have stretched your authority and fear upon us long enough! My dear best friend is in a life or death situation! We need to get out of here, and the only thing that is standing in our way is you! Now, are you with us or are you against us?"

"I..."

"If you do plan on stopping us or tattle tailing like a little child, we need to know. Otherwise, do yourself a favor and get us some torches for when we go outside."

Amelia had never heard anything like that come from Mary. Agatha, who did not seem to come up with anything else, just stood there, mouth opened in shock. "There are some torches downstairs near the gates," she replied softly. "We can get them on the way out."

"All right," Daleen said, "Let us go."

And with that, Mary began to walk up front. Then, Daleen and Amelia were in the middle, and Agatha and Elizabeth were behind. Everyone looked around before they left the room to make sure that they did not leave anything behind. Then, as soon as everyone left the room, Elizabeth closed the doors.

Chapter 8:

Leaving Arigog

With extreme caution, they quietly crept down the long hallway. While walking, Amelia looked around. The hallway, to her surprise, had various paintings and sculptures all over the walls. On one side, there was a painting of the palace, surrounded by red flower bushes and a tall Vase on a pedestal by itself. On the other side, there was a painting of a king and a queen Amelia had never met before. She guessed that it was probably one of her ancestors who passed long before she was born. Next to it was a painting of a scarlet dragon on a mountain, blowing its fire at silver knights. It was very amusing. Amelia had passed these halls for years, but she never noticed any of this, and now she didn't have any time to enjoy it. After they had passed the hall, they began to walk down the stairs. Elizabeth had skipped a step and Amelia nearly slipped on the way down. As they were passing the ballroom, Amelia wanted to glance inside, but the doors were shut and she was quite glad about it. After they passed the throne room, they walked through the opened doors and out of the palace. It was incredibly dark outside except for the stars glistening in the night sky.

Amelia looked around, and to her surprise, no one was outside. "Where are the guards?"

"I do not know," Daleen answered, "Perhaps they are looking for you. My goodness, it is dark. Agatha, where are the torches?"

"They are over here."

Agatha left and came back with a few torches as she headed over to a lit torch hanging on the wall. She took one and lit it on fire. Then, she did it to the others one by one, handing them out until everyone except Amelia and Daleen had one in their hand.

"That's enough torches," said Daleen, "We don't need too much light. Some of the people are sleeping already and may cause attention to ourselves."

"What are you talking about?" Agatha asked.

"We need to be incognito, not having enough torches to look as if we are starting a riot."

"Good point."

As they walked on the wide drawbridge, Amelia looked over, seeing the river below them as it showed her blurry reflection.

The air was cool, and the streets were not as flat as the floors inside the palace. The homes in the town were structured and built perfectly. While walking, one of the lit houses caught Amelia's eye. After all, she lived in the palace her entire life and had never seen what the houses looked like inside. Amelia got out of Daleen's grip and rushed to the house.

"Princess," Daleen whispered, "Princess, what are you doing? We must go."

"Wait. Please, I wish to see this." She quickly ran toward the house and peeked inside one of the windows.

Inside was a family, with what looked like friends and servants, enjoying a meal. The men were on one side of a rectangular table, laughing to their heart's content. The women were next to them, either giggling or just smiling. On the other side were the children, both boys and girls, eating their food. Amelia then looked at the youngest girl. She looked about four and was in a lovely pink dress. While the other children were eating, she was just sitting there with a miserable look on her face. Instead of facing her plate, she was looking away toward a wall. There sitting in a corner was a broken doll dressed as if she was going to a ball. The girl, not being able to take the separation anymore, tried to get up from her seat in an attempt to retrieve her damaged toy. No sooner than she did, a woman whom Amelia guessed to be her mother turned her head straight at the girl and gave a nasty scowl. The girl, who read the facial message immediately, sat back in her seat and lowered her head. The mother looked satisfied as she continued to smile at the other women.

"What is it, my dear?" Daleen had walked up to Amelia.

"Nothing," Amelia said, "It is nothing." Daleen then walked away, and Amelia took one last look inside before walking away as well. The girl still was sad as she stared at her doll in the corner.

After what had felt like ten minutes, they passed the last of the houses and finally made it to the Revel Forest. Standing in front of them were hundreds of tall, green trees with a narrow dirt path inside.

"Maybe we should turn back," Agatha said, "Now, before it is too late. After all, the forest is dangerous."

"Agatha," Daleen replied, "It is only dangerous because of the Slavernors. Do not listen to her, Princess. We speak of Slavernors to scare children into not entering the forest; however, there are such people around in the woods. Just move during the daytime and stay hidden at night. I am sure that you will be all right."

"But would it not be best if I was to move at night?"

"Actually, they are capable of attacking at any time of the day. Besides, with this cloak, it will be hard for you to be seen in the dark."

Amelia then took a few steps and looked inside the forest, and then she looked back at the others. "I wish to thank you all for everything. I do not wish for you all to be in any more danger, so when you do not see me anymore in the distance, head back to the palace." She then proceeded to hug Elizabeth, even Agatha, and then she gave Mary a tight hug. "Farewell, Mary. You have truly been a great friend." Mary's eyes began to fill with tears as they let go. "And thank you most of all, Daleen." She went and hugged Daleen one last time. For that moment, Amelia enjoyed the warmth of the hug, and then, before she could even think, she felt a kiss on her forehead.

Amelia then took the bag from Elizabeth and began to walk. She turned around and took one last look at them. These fine women had helped her in her time of need. Words could not describe how thankful she was for the fact that they took an incredible risk just for her. Amelia then turned around, placed the hood on her head, and entered the dark forest.

Chapter 9:

The Revel Forest

Amelia walked deeper into the forest as her maids and Mary left. As she walked, she kept glancing back as the light from their torches disappeared. It was almost like seeing a sunset. Then, when she could not see their light anymore, she hastened her pace and never looked back. For what felt like an hour, she kept a steady pace on the path. Her lonely footsteps were drowned out by the sounds of nature, as if every tree and creature in the forest thought that tonight would be the perfect night to make noises. Amelia then tried to create thoughts that would get her mind off of the sounds.

She imagined Mary, probably feeling good that of all of the "friends" Amelia had, she was chosen as the truest. Amelia thought of Daleen and how worried she must be. It must be scary to know that her princess, whom she had practically raised, is now going into a dangerous forest alone. Amelia then thought of her parents, with her mother being mortified and her father being furious. She regretted thinking that as fear returned with this fact. The fact that the guards will be ordered by the King to bring the Princess back into the ballroom, only to find her missing. The fact that they will take their torches and swords and storm out of the castle. The fact that they may find Mary and the maids to take them and question them about the location of their Princess. The fact that they will hunt for the Princess and perhaps take her to her execution. Her heart began to sink like a rock underwater at this thought. She now felt as if every tree in the forest was leaning and closing in on her as if they were guards with their swords held high, waiting for the command to strike.

Then, she stopped as a small sound filled the air, one that stood out above all the others. Was it the guards already? Did they actually squeeze the information out of Agatha that easily? Amelia stood perfectly still, closed her eyes, and listened closely to the sound.

Grumble, grumble, grumble!

Amelia held her stomach and laughed. "It is only me."

Grumble, grumble, grumble!

She laughed as she realized that she had forgotten to eat. She was so distraught over the party and Vase that she didn't even eat a single bite. She looked for a spot to rest and found a green patch of grass with little flowers. "I guess this shall suffice for tonight." Amelia sat down in the soft patch, then she opened the bag and took out a wrapped up piece of cooked sheep and bread. Despite the fact that it was in the old bag for a while, the food was still warm. After that, she washed it down with some water. Now feeling safe and satisfied, she laid down, using the cloak as a blanket, and went to sleep.

When dawn rose, Amelia woke up confused. Then she remembered the night before and relaxed, realizing where she was. She then ate some of her food and continued her journey. For several days, Amelia walked down the path, which seemed to be never-ending. To make herself feel comfortable, she made herself a routine. In the morning, she would wake up at the crack of dawn, eat, and then walk. She also did not eat lunch to save her food, which was beginning to decrease. Despite the fact that she was being pursued by royal guards, she was happy as she wandered the forest. At night, she would find a spot to rest, eat again, and go to sleep. She did this day in and day out, adapting more and more to her surroundings.

As the sun went down on her fifth day in the forest, Amelia felt exhaustion take over. She was covered with sweat and filth and her arms, legs, and face received small cuts from being snagged by the trees. Her new and once beautiful red dress was torn from the bottom and was so dirty that it was starting to look maroon. This, however, did not bother her considering that she hated this dress and could not wait to find something else to wear just to take it off. She felt willing to even wear men's clothes if it meant that she could remove this tight and uncomfortable excuse of clothing. Seeing that it was getting late, she started to look for a place to rest for the night.

Instead of finding any form of a comfortable place, she found a large boulder that was halfway covered in green moss. Touching the boulder was a large tree with a deep crack on its side, as if it was gnawed by a beaver. As Amelia looked at the boulder and tree, her eyes caught the sky. It was filled with giant, dark clouds, making it seem as if it was getting ready to rain. She knew that a patch of grass or leaves wouldn't work tonight, and she definitely knew that the cloak was not impervious to water. She needed to find shelter and fast. But what could she do? She was in the middle of the forest with nowhere to go. While she was scrambling for a form of cover, her eyes caught something else.

The sunset reflected off of something under the leaves just ahead, blinding her. She quickly went over, removed the leaves, and lifted up the object, revealing a sharp sword. It looked as if it was new and had a large and rectangular red jewel on both sides of the hilt. She then had a crazy idea. She knew that it was not an ax, but it was going to have to do. Amelia dropped the bag and cloak. Then, she picked up the sword, which was very light-weight, and went toward the tree and aimed at the deep cut. She lifted the sword high and swung it into the tree. She repeatedly swung the sword as the cut was getting deeper until . . .

Crrreeaaakkk!!!!!!

To her surprise, her plan worked. From where the tree was hit, it began to fall as Amelia quickly got out of the way.

Boom!

As the sound of a falling tree faded and was replaced by that of rustling leaves, Amelia looked at what she had done. The tree had torn, and the fallen half was lying on the ground, creating a triangular shaped cave. Before Amelia could continue to admire her work, she felt a raindrop. The rain began its fall as Amelia quickly grabbed the bag, cloak, and sword and entered the new cave.

Chapter 10:

Sweet Rest

Within minutes, the rain turned into a storm as now lightening filled the sky. However, because of Amelia's quick thinking, the tree collected all of the raindrops while she stayed warm and dry. Curious about the object that helped with the work, Amelia took the sword to get a closer look. The sword was covered in dirt and pieces of wood, but it still looked new. Amelia then realized that the hilt did not actually have jewels, but large red letters. On one side of the hilt, the name "Shaw" was printed. On the other side, in bigger letters, were the initials "R.T.S.". Amelia had never heard of anyone with the initial "R.T.S," and who was this Shaw? Nevertheless, Amelia was grateful that their sword was here for her to use it. To celebrate her great accomplishment, she went into the bag to find some food. Unfortunately, there was not much left.

The once great bounty of food had shrunk over the days. Amelia took out what looked the freshest: half a jug of water, some meat, and what looked like a small dried loaf of bread. Everything else in the bag had already started to mold to the point that Amelia couldn't even tell what half of the things were. Amelia closed the bag and placed it aside, knowing that she would have to find a way to get food and water tomorrow. She began to eat the meat, which she guessed was cooked cattle. She then washed it down with a little bit of water. Then, with a bit of hesitation, she picked up the bread and took a bite. *It is . . . sweet?* Amelia thought as she looked inside the food. Instead of seeing a dry texture seen in the insides of bread, there were sliced apples in a sugary filling. *An . . . an apple tart? They had managed to sneak an apple tart?* She thought about this for a while, and then she smiled and took another bite. The sweet flavor reminded her of her childhood.

She remembered having her first apple tart when she was four. She was strolling into the kitchen when she noticed Daleen rolling dough. "Hello, Daleen. What are you doing?" asked four-year-old Amelia.

"Oh! Good morning, Princess," Daleen replied, "I am making apple tarts. They are very soft and sweet. Would you like one?" She outstretched her arm, picked up a warm, golden brown tart from a nearby plate, and presented it to Amelia, who slowly grabbed it and took a bite.

"Mmmmmmmm! This is yummy, Daleen."

"Why thank you, Princess. They are very easy to make. First, you must get some sliced apples. Then you mix it with spices, honey, and love. Then you place it in sweet pastry dough and cook it over a fire." As she said that, she went towards the kitchen fire and placed tarts onto a plate. "If you like, you can have as many as you please." The child's smile widened as she grabbed another apple tart and took a bite.

Boom!

Amelia came back to focus as the sound of thunder returned her from her flashback. She looked down at the tart, thinking about Daleen and hoping that her favorite maid was alight. She smiled at this thought as she finished the tart and drank the rest of the water. She took the bag, emptied it and crawled a little closer to the boulder. She placed the bag on the ground so that way the cleanest part could be used as a pillow. Using the cloak as a blanket, she laid her head down. She then closed her eyes and went to sleep.

"Careful with that." A grouchy, heavy voice woke Amelia hours later from her sleep. Was it the guards already? Have they found the lost princess to take her to her death? And why does it sound as if one of them is in a bad mood? Then there was silence. Perhaps it was a sound she was hearing from her dream. Amelia thought of this as she lay her head back down to go to sleep . . .

Boom!

There was the sound of an impact of metal to ground that was so hard and loud that it shocked Amelia and even made the earth beneath her shake. "I said be careful! You have no idea how long it took me to get this!"

"Keep your voice down, I'm trying," replied a different grouchy voice. "It's heavy, and your horse is out of control. Easy, *easy!*" The sound of a horse filled the air as Amelia peeked out of her cave to find the source of the ruckus.

Standing yards away, Amelia could see two men on the path. They were struggling to calm down a horse, which was pulling a large object with torches. "Come on. Leave it here. We need to catch up with the others before we hunt. We can come back and get it when we're done." They each took torches and began to walk off the path and in Amelia's direction. She could hear the sound of leaves as the men's footsteps were getting closer and closer.

"Whoa! Look at this tree. That storm must have struck it down."

"Keep *your* voice down! Do you want the whole land to hear you?" The footsteps of the heavy-voiced man stopped a few feet away from the tree and Amelia. "Yeah, the storm must've done that. Let's keep moving. I want to get this done quickly."

"Hey, don't you think someone would steal our stuff? We are far away from it now."

"No, you idiot, you would need the key first."

"Where is it?"

"None of your business. It's in a place far away, so that way fools like you won't cause damage."

"For the last time, I don't know what happened."

"You've managed to push the whole thing off the cliff and you still can't tell me what happened? Well, this time I'm making sure it doesn't happen again." Their arguing continued as the sound of the footsteps died.

Amelia panicked and began to fill the bag with the food. She then remembered that all of the food that she had taken out was molded, so there was no longer a need for the food or the bag. Realizing this, she placed the bag back on the ground. When Amelia could no longer hear them or see the light of their torches, she placed the hood over her head and crawled out of the cave. She walked on the path as quickly and quietly as possible. Then, she hid behind a tree to see what was blocking the path. Alone in the middle of the path was a tall, tan horse, pulling a giant iron cage on wheels. Whoever these men were, Amelia knew that they were not guards. But they were a danger for her and she needed to get out of here.

"Hey! Who's there?"

Amelia turned around. A figure with his torch held high stood on top of a small hill. Amelia looked closer at the figure and saw, to her horror, iron shackles strapped to his belt. With fear consuming her, Amelia whispered to herself. "Slavernors."

Chapter 11:

Dangers in the Forest

Amelia took a long look at the man. Then, without hesitation, she slowly backed up and then broke into a run.

"Hey! We have a trespasser!"

Almost instantly, the sound of men and their footsteps filled the air. Amelia ran as fast as she could, but as she did so, she came to the realization that she was being followed. The lights from the torches were almost making it seem like sunlight as more Slavernors appeared out of nowhere. She kept running for what felt like several minutes, making sure to hasten her pace and to avoid looking back. Then after a long time, she hid behind a tree to catch her breath. She looked around to see if she was still being followed. The light of the torches were far away, but Amelia could not tell if the light was coming closer or moving away. She stood there, surrounded in darkness and absolute silence. Then she took a deep sigh, feeling quite safe at the moment . . .

Thud!

Amelia looked up. Inches away from her head was an arrow, deeply implanted into the bark of the tree. She quickly broke into a run again as she heard more arrows barely miss her. It felt as if every footprint she made was replaced with an arrow or two. Then, she saw a large tree that had fallen and was in her way. It was too tall and would take too much time to climb, so Amelia tried to look for the end to go around it. "Argh!"

Just before she got close to it, Amelia tripped over a tree root and fell face first into the ground. She got onto her knees, attempting to catch her breath and hoping that no one heard her fall. She tried to prepare herself to run again.

But as she tried to get up, something cold touched her forehead. When she lifted her head, a long, sharp sword was right in front of her, inches away from her nose. She then slowly lifted her head to see the wielder.

Standing on top of the tree was a man whom she could tell was a Slavernor. He had a long and curly red beard and hair, and his clothes were so filthy that Amelia could barely tell what they were. He had an aggressive look on his face, which was covered in marks. His right eye was green, but his other eye was white with a very deep scar. The man took the sword away from Amelia's face and into the cloak.

Then, still using the sword, he pushed the hood off of her head. The man's face changed into a look of awe as he gazed at her. Then he smiled, showing his teeth, which were either yellow, black, or gone. "Well, hello, pretty lady," he said as he lifted the sword away. Amelia realized that this was the man with the heavy voice from earlier. "You look lost. Here, let me help you." And with that, he jumped off the tree, placed his sword away, grabbed Amelia by her cloak, and dragged her all the way back to the cage. "Hey," he shouted, "look what I've found." He then threw her onto the ground. Amelia sat herself up as more than twenty Slavernors surrounded her.

"Well, well, well," said another Slavernor, "You caught one. And she's a beauty. Good job, Gremeak!" The man then stood tall as he ran his fingers through his red beard with pride. Amelia realized that this man was the other guy with the grouchy voice. "Sooo . . . " the Slavernor said as he stepped back. "What should we do with her? I say we rob her. I'm sure she has something valuable under that cloak."

"Or . . . " said a blond-haired Slavernor. "We could bruise her up. I say we destroy her pretty little face."

"I say we could just go and have a little fun with her," said a black-haired Slavernor, "And if she tries to resist, we could easily shut her up." As he said this, he took out his sword and pointed it at Amelia.

"Well," Gremeak replied as he shooed the sword away, "those are good ideas. But, as always, I have a better idea. I say we take her into the market and give her as a slave to Jack."

All the Slavernors looked up at Gremeak, looking both surprised and terrified. "Jack," the blond-haired Slavernor asked, "You mean *the* Jack?"

"Yep," Gremeak replied, "I know him personally. He and I are close friends. She would make a perfect gift. Let's put her in the cage."

Before Amelia could do anything, she was lifted off the ground. Gremeak then walked to the cage, placed his hand into this clothing, and took out a key.

"So that's where it was." said the grouchy-voiced Slavernor.

"Just shut up."

Gremeak unlocked and opened the door. Amelia was thrown inside and Gremeak locked the door. She got up and tried to get out, but it was no use. She could hear the Slavernors laughing as the cage began to move. She tried to calm herself down by sitting down and closing her eyes. She tried to imagine that this was all a terrible dream. She imagined herself in the palace, safe and sound. When she opened her eyes, she was still sitting on iron.

After a few minutes went by, Amelia's mind began to feel numb. She could not believe that this was happening. A few days ago, she had broken her Vase after saying no to a proposal. Now, she was captured by Slavernors and trapped in a cage, about to be given as a slave. And who is this "Jack" that they were talking about? She had never heard of a man with that name, and yet it brought fear to the Slavernors' faces. The thing she was afraid to figure out was why. What is so scary about a man named Jack? Amelia continued to ponder this for a few minutes, overwhelming herself with what he may look like. She imagined a large, terrifying man with a large sword and his body drenched in blood, blood that may soon be her own. With fear and exhaustion taking over her, Amelia dragged herself into a corner and cried herself to sleep.

Chapter 12:

The Marketplace

The morning sun and the sound of clamoring people were synchronized as Amelia woke up in the cell. She slowly got up, aching in pain from her uncomfortable slumber, and went to the door. Outside was an enormous market with large tents as far as her eyes could see with merchants selling their stuff in the dirt street. In one tent, a plump woman was giving gold coins to a man in exchange for a basket of fruits.

In another tent, a tall man was holding cloaks in his arms. "Buy fabrics here," he shouted, "Buy fabrics here! From linen to the fanciest cotton! Five gold coins each!" There was even a tent full of caged animals. Inside a few of these cages were birds, dogs, and even a monkey. However, as the ride continued, the market had a dark transition.

The tents of fruits and cloths were replaced with tents of more caged animals, weapons, and then chained people. Amelia saw an old man on the ground in chains and brutally beaten. Nearby was a woman cleaning her feet next to a bucket of water. But before Amelia could observe anymore, the cage had come to a halt.

"Ugh! Finally!" said one of the Slavernors, "It felt like eternity to get here. So, where do you think Jack is?"

"I'll find him," Gremeak replied, "he's usually at the tavern waiting for a bounty or a job to do." And with that, Amelia heard the sound of Gremeak getting off of the carriage and walking away. As the sound of his footsteps died, Amelia looked at her surroundings.

They had stopped right next to a large tan tent that had several female slaves in a cage. There was a woman who appeared to be in a very bad mood. Another one was standing with a posture as if she was looking for a fight. There was even a little girl with the look of dirt and innocence on her face. Suddenly, Amelia heard the footsteps of Gremeak and, to her horror, of someone else.

"Over here, Jack," Gremeak said, "I think you'll like what I have for you."

"It better be worth it," replied a new voice, "I was just about to finish a deal. The guy is in a relationship with a married woman and she wants her husband dead. They were offering me a lot of money, too."

"I promise you Jack that this is well worth it. And if it's not, I'll give you the amount of money that they were offering."

The footsteps became louder and louder as they stopped at the door of the cage. Amelia could see the shadows of two figures welcoming themselves through the bars.

Click! Boom! Shreeeech!

Amelia jumped against the wall as the door was unlocked and opened. The sun began to blind her as a figure came up to her.

"Come on now. I don't have all day." Amelia felt herself being grabbed and tossed into the light. She flew out of the cage and onto the ground. As she scrambled to her feet, she looked up and saw this Jack.

Instead of being the terrifying killer Amelia had imagined, Jack looked more like a handsome prince. He was a tall brown-haired man wearing a white shirt, a brown vest, and boots. Despite the small scars, he had an angel-sculpted complexion that made a very admirable face.

"Well, what do you think?" asked Gremeak.

Jack gave a look of disgust, but as Amelia stood up, their eyes met. Amelia tried to look away, but she couldn't help but look. In shock of her actual appearance, Jack's eyes widened, and to Amelia's surprise, were revealed to be hazel.

"She's beautiful, isn't she? But I see you don't want her, so I could just..."

"I'll take her."

"What?"

"I said I'll take her."

"Oh. All right. In that case, she's all yours . . ."

"Not so fast," said a different voice, "If you want her, you'll have to pay. That'll be six hundred coins. In fact, make it seven hundred because of her pretty looks."

Inside the big tent was a skinny man, standing behind a table. Gremeak began to walk towards the slave salesman. Jack then grabbed Amelia by her arm and did the same. Unlike the harsh gestures made by the other Slavernors, Jack's grip was firm, but at the same time gentle.

"What did you say to me?" Jack asked when they had reached the table.

"You heard me," the man replied, "Seven hundred coins for the girl. The cage is parked next to *my* tent; therefore, the cage, horse, and girl are mine. Now, I'm only saying this one more time: that'll be seven hundred coins. Take it or leave it."

"And what if I say I want her for free."

"No! Seven hundred coins!"

"Hey," Gremeak shouted, "first of all, let me warn you, this is *the* Jack you are talking to, so keep the attitude down."

"I know who he is quite well. Although some of the things he has been said to do are a little exaggerated."

"Second," Gremeak said, completely ignoring the man's sentence, "your slaves usually cost four hundred coins. Besides, she wasn't even in a tent, so what makes you think you can claim her?"

"Because I can! Now, she's seven hundred coins, and I'm not changing it! Not for you, the girl, or for this bastard right here!" The slave salesman moved himself into Jack's face, which was starting to turn red with anger. "Do you hear me, pretty boy? I'm not changing the price, and you can't make me! Do you hear me, little boy? I would rather die than to let this deal down! Augghhh!"

Everyone stood still as everything happened at once. Jack had let go of Amelia, pushed her aside, and went into his belt. He retrieved a dagger as he grabbed the salesman's hair. Then, he lifted the dagger behind him and, with all of his might, swung it right into the man's neck. Everyone around and watching Jack jumped in shock as the man immediately began to couch up blood.

Jack slowly opened his mouth and said, "Then die already."

Jack snatched the dagger from the man's neck as he fell to the ground, choking on his own blood. More blood poured out from his throat as he twitched for a few seconds. Then, he slowly stopped twitching with his eyes wide opened as he lay there, never to get up again.

Did he . . . did he just . . . kill him? Amelia thought.

Meanwhile, Jack went back into his pocket, pulled out a brown rag and began to clean the blade.

"My, Jack, your stuff is filthy. It looks like you really do need a slave."

"I guess I do need someone other than me to get certain things done." Jack said as he placed the dagger into his belt and placed the rag back into his pocket.

"Well," Gremeak said as he walked past the body and to the other slaves, "I guess they belong to us now? Which ones do you want, Jack?"

"All of them."

"Pardon me."

"I want all of them. After all," he began to speak in a deep tone, mocking the dead salesman, "the salesman was killed by *my* blade. So the slaves, goods, and the tent are mine now. I'm sure that there is something here that's valuable."

Gremeak looked as if he was going to speak against this, but he looked at the body again and said, "All right. Fair enough. Let's load up and go."

Jack walked around the table with his face still red with rage. He went to the body, took a set of keys and handed them to Gremeak, who unlocked the cell and herded all of the slaves out.

"As of now, you are all my slaves. Do as I say and you live. If you don't, well . . . I think you understand. Now, as my first command, I want you all to take this tent down and load it and the goods, if any, to the cage."

Almost immediately, the slaves had spread out and went to work. Amelia came back into focus and, making sure that she wasn't his next victim, walked away and did the same. Amelia, to be honest, had no idea what she was doing, but as she pulled the ropes of the tent, it began to loosen. Within minutes, the tent was wrapped up.

Suddenly, Gremeak had let out an enormous laugh. "Ha! Ha! Jack! You were right. Look!"

Behind the cages, in what was supposed to be the back of the tent, were the supposed goods. There was food, large barrels of wine, clothing, even gold coins and furniture. All of the Slavernors were shouting with joy as the slaves began to load the stuff. As Amelia helped pick up a table, she overheard Jack say, "Now this is definitely worth my deal."

Chapter 13:

Forest of Concealment

After everything was loaded, the slaves went into the cage. They sat down quietly with their backs against the walls, surrounded by stuff as the cage began to move. Amelia looked outside. The area where the tent had been was now gone and the only thing left was the salesman in the heat.

"Please do not tell me that we shall leave the poor man's dead body behind," Amelia said. "Surely these men are not that harsh."

"Well," said a slave, "unfortunately, they are."

Amelia stood there in disbelief, then turned around and watched as the man's body disappeared from view. Everyone was quiet as hours passed. The scenery changed as they left the marketplace and into a forest.

"Does anyone know where we are?" Amelia asked after a long time of silence.

"We're in the Forest of Concealment," said a slave. "It's the biggest forest in the land. It's the perfect place to get lost, or in this case, stay hidden. There's a field in the middle of the forest that no one goes through because they say Jack uses it as a hideout. We're probably heading there."

As more hours passed, the trees were getting thicker and the sun was going down. Then, at long last, the cage finally came to a stop. A few seconds later, the sound of footsteps came and got louder and louder as a figure opened the door, with Gremeak standing on the other side. "All right. Get out here and make the tents and dinner."

He left as the slaves got up, picked up as much stuff as they could carry, and exited the cage. They, as the slave had said earlier, were in a large field surrounded by trees and a flowing river nearby. Some of the slaves went and began collecting water from the river while the rest began putting up the tents.

Within an hour, the tents were up, water was collected, and the meals were made. After Amelia had put the hammer for the tents away, she followed a few slaves to what she guessed was their tent. The tent, like most of the others, was dark green with dirt and small patches on its sides. The inside looked comfortable, with enough space for all of them to fit with room to spare. The beds were lined together, each with animal skins on top. Most of the slaves in the room were huddled together in front of a bed. As Amelia approached them, one of them noticed her and looked up. She looked about Amelia's age with green eyes and her brown hair tied up in a long braid.

"Oh, hello," she said, "Come over here. We have new clothes."

Amelia hurried herself over to the huddle. The clothes that the slave was referring to was a heap of brown, raggedy dresses, shoes and thin belts.

"We found them while taking down the tent. They don't look as if they were worn, and there should be enough for all of us. Here, try this one on." The slave picked up one of the dresses and handed it to Amelia, who took it and walked to one of the other beds. As she began to take off her dress, she struggled as the strings were in a tight knot. The slave who gave her the dress saw Amelia struggling and walked towards her. "Here," she said, "Let me help. Loosening dresses by yourself can be difficult."

Amelia turned around and the slave began to untie the knot. Within seconds, the slave was able to untie the uncomfortable dress, which, for Amelia, was a great relief.

Amelia took off her dress and began putting on the other one. The slave then gave her a belt and shoes. The outfit was not the type of clothing Amelia would usually wear, but it was one of the most comfortable things she had ever worn. "By the way," the slave said, "My name is Murean. Murean Hatchet."

"I am thankful for your help, Murean," Amelia replied with a smile.

They then walked to the huddle, which during their time of changing, had now moved to the entrance of the tent. They were all crowding a black pot on top of a fire, where small bowls of stew were being passed around. A bowl was given to another slave, then to Murean, and then to Amelia. After everyone in the tent had a bowl, they selected a bed and began to eat. Amelia picked her bed and sat down as Murean, now being more friendly, sat on the bed next to her. She looked into her bowl of food, which smelled odd and had what looked like chucks of meat and vegetables in an ugly brown liquid that was lighter than her dress. It did not look appetizing, but she was willing to eat it, considering she hadn't eaten since she was captured. With a bit of hesitation, she picked up the spoon and ate some of the stew. Despite the ugly look and odd smell, the stew was delicious. She began to eat to the point that she almost forgot her manners as she shoveled spoonful after spoonful. Murean, who now noticed her new friend, looked surprised and a little scared.

"Goodness! Are you hungry? You're eating as if you haven't had food in days."

"Forgive me," Amelia replied, "most of the food that I have had for days was old. I also was captured a day ago and I have not received food until now. Besides, this food is very tasty."

"Why, thank you," said an older slave. "I'm sure that we have enough for seconds. The slave salesman has enough food to feed a small army. Oh, where are my manners? My name is Edith. I was captured during a raid five years ago, and I've been a slave ever since."

"That's nothing," replied another slave. "My name is Tama. I've been sold as almost every kind of slave. I've been a servant, a guard, and even a fighter. Being a fighter was the best one. I killed so many people during competitions, even my last slave master before I was captured again."

Suddenly, there was a petty laugh. "How simply barbaric," said a voice. "In my land, we would never allow such disgusting behavior."

Sitting near the entrance was a black-haired girl, sitting tall on her bed with an air of elegance, as if she was sitting on a throne. She, like Murean, looked as if she was Amelia's age with fair skin and rosy cheeks. She was also wearing a smile and, as Amelia noticed, a necklace with a purple phoenix on it.

"And who are you?" Murean asked. The slave stood up tall with her head held up high with pride, reminding Amelia of her people in Arigog.

"I am Delilah, loyal citizen of Destera."

"Ugh! A Destramech," said Tama. "And what do you do in your land?"

"We learn life lessons through difficult trials, such as obedience and loyalty to our masters, even if they do happen to be bounty hunters. That is why I have stayed with all of my masters."

"Well, you can be loyal to them as long as you want. Just don't do anything stupid when we escape."

"Escape?" asked Amelia.

"Yes," Tama replied. "We do plan on getting out of here. We already had a plan made out and a leader to help us get it done."

"And who is this leader?" asked Delilah.

"Anna," Tama replied, looking in her opposite direction.

There on the other side of the tent was a blonde-haired young woman sitting on her bed. She had managed to be so quiet that Amelia was just noticing her there. She had a small scar on her cheek, and she had a stern look on her face, as if she was ready to kill at any moment. The second her name was called, she stood up and walked toward them. "I'll make this quick. My name's Anna, and I'm the leader. You do as I recommend, you'll live. If you don't, you'll die. End of story."

"We were going to escape today at nightfall," said Tama, "but when Jack showed up, we knew that it was over. We could still use it though. You see, all we have to do is..."

"Actually, there is a change of plans."

"What?"

"Yes. This whole trying to escape thing is not going to work. I think that we are just going to do what Delilah says and serve the masters."

"What? Bu—"

"I'm the leader, and as leader of this group, I say that we will do this instead."

Delilah gave a look of shock and joy. "Well," she said with excitement, "this is truly delightful. You know, Anna, you have made an excellent decision. Most people that I was enslaved with tried to escape. And do you know how they are now? Dead, simply dead. You, however, have understood quickly, and for that I congratulate you."

"Thanks." Anna replied. "You wouldn't happen to know what they might have us doing, would you? It's been a while since I've been a servant."

"Ah, yes. When the sun rises, we must make breakfast. Then later, we must make lunch and dinner. At the same time, we must clean the clothes, clean their weapons, get wood and food, and do whatever the masters ask us to do. The masters usually don't care who does it, as long as they get it done."

"Thanks. We can figure out who does what later."

Delilah then got up and headed for the tent flap. "Now, if you shall excuse me, I must go see what they desire. I shall see you all later. Farewell." She then left the tent.

Tama, who was still in shock, turned her head to the entrance and then to Anna.

"So, this is it? After all that has happened to us, this is the new plan?"

Anna gave a small laugh. "No. I just said all of that to get little-miss-perfect out of here. She doesn't seem like a person who can keep secrets."

"So, we're still going with the plan?"

"No. We're still changing it."

"Why? The plan is fine. It doesn't need to be changed."

"Well, now there's a reason for it to be changed."

As she said this, she picked up a bowl and began to eat. "The original plan was to lure the salesman to the cage so that way we could knock him out and get the key. When we first had this idea, our only obstacles were the cage and the slave salesman. Now, we have bounty hunters and Jack. We were escaping for our freedom, but now we need to escape for our lives or we will die here. We need a new one, but first, we need to know what we are up against. I only know a few hunters."

"I know a few of them," Murean said. "First, there's Lance, the young-looking one with the clean boots. He's a new hunter. Then, there's Montague . . ."

"He's scary," interrupted a small voice.

A small, light-skinned girl was sitting on her bed with a filthy doll in her arms.

"Who is she?" asked Amelia.

"That's Mila," said Tama, "She's four, and Montague isn't really scary, but he is crazy. When his village was attacked by a foreign army, he was able to sneak into their camp. A few hours later, the leader and half of the army was killed. Limbs were horribly cut off, and some of them just bled to death. It was a bloodbath."

The thought of it sent chills down Amelia's spine.

"Then, there's Gremeak," said Anna.

"The bearded Slavernor?" Amelia asked.

"Yes. He's a great bounty hunter, and he has captured hundreds of people, including me."

"I was captured by him a year ago," said Murean, "And then . . . there's Jack."

Sighs filled the room as they expressed fear on their faces.

"That," Anna said, "I'm afraid is our main problem. If we can't get past him, we're doomed."

"Umm . . . who is this Jack?"

Everyone in the tent nearly broke their necks as they stared at Amelia. Murean looked scared, Anna nearly spilled her food, and Mila dropped her jaw.

"You don't know?" Murean asked. "You don't *know* who *Jack* is?"

"No."

"How do you not know who he is?" Anna asked

"I have never heard of him where I am from."

After a few seconds, Murean came back to focus and said, "Jack Vernono, from the land of Merrigan, is the deadliest man in the land!"

"And don't let his looks deceive you," Tama added. "He's wanted all over the lands as the most dangerous bounty hunter that has ever lived."

"It's true," said Edith. "This man is capable of killing people with anything. He can kill with swords, random objects, his bare hands, anything!"

"Years ago," Tama said, "he was eating a meal at a tavern. In fact, I think it was the same tavern near the marketplace. Anyway, he was about to finish his plate, which only had bread left, when a drunken man started shouting at him. The verbal fight soon got physical, and somehow it moved outside. Well, the people inside were about to go out to see the fight continue when they heard a loud scream. There was a long silence before someone went out to find the source of the sound. The person came back, pale as a ghost and unable to say a word. Everyone emptied the tavern to find the drunken man a few yards away, dead."

"Dead?"

"Yes. The man had multiple wounds and a fork stabbed into his throat. When the people returned to the tavern, Jack's plate was found empty."

Anna, still confused, asked, "You said that you never heard of him where you are from?"

"Yes."

"Where are you from, anyway?"

"Arigog."

"Who are you?"

"My name is Amelia. I am the daughter of William Asselin, Princess of Arigog."

"What?" everyone said in unison.

"Are you really the princess?" asked Murean.

"Yes."

"Prove it."

"She already did," said Edith.

"How?"

"Well, because of how she refers to the hunters as "Slavernors," because all that they do around her land is capture people."

"Bu-but . . . what are you doing here," Tama asked. "Aren't you supposed to be in a fancy palace or something?"

"I ran away, and then I was captured."

"Why did you run away?" Mila asked.

"I . . . I broke my Vase."

Both Tama and Anna looked confused.

"A what?" Anna asked. "What's so scary about a vase?"

"I know what she's talking about," said Edith. "In Arigog, the high society people have these Vases that foretell their lives, and they have to follow it to the letter, and if they don't, they are executed. But . . . that usually never happens. Most people, as I know it, enjoy what their Vase has foretold for them, and if they get broken, it's usually by accident. Why did you break yours?"

"I was supposed to marry a man that I never even liked."

"Would you mind telling us about it?"

And so Amelia told them about everything that she could tell them, about not only the Vase, but of her entire life. She told them about her hatred of the Vase, the proposal, and the destruction of the Vase. "And so," Amelia finished, "with the Vase completely beyond repair, I had to run away and leave Arigog."

When she finished, there was a moment of silence, and at the same time, Amelia felt relived. She had never really told anyone about this other than Mary and Daleen, and now that she had, she felt as if a great weight was lifted from her chest.

"Ummm," said Anna, "so . . . does this mean that we have to address you in a fancy way, like the High Royalty Princess or Your Great Highness?"

"No . . . call me . . . Amelia . . . just Amelia."

"Well, just Amelia, I never thought that someone would be capable of doing what you did. Yet again, I never thought that I would ever meet the princess of Arigog as a slave."

Amelia gave a small smile at that remark. "Yes. But I suppose my actions were a little foolish."

"No. It wasn't foolish. In fact, I think it was quite brave of you."

"Really?"

"Yes. It takes pure guts to go against what you were told was right, even if it means to go against your own family. You know, Amelia, at first I almost thought that you were like little-miss-perfect, but now I know that you're different. As far as I'm concerned, you have my liking and respect."

"Thank you."

"No problem. Just don't try to lose it. A lot of people do." Anna finished her food, placed the bowl on her bed, and headed for the tent flap. "Oh, and you might want to keep the whole princess thing to yourself. Many people here would have a happy day if they were to find out that they have royalty as a slave." And with that, she left without saying another word.

Chapter 14:

First Day

The sun was high in the sky the next morning as Amelia felt Murean waking her up.

"Good morning, Amelia."

"Hmmmm . . . good morning."

"Come on. I need help cleaning weapons."

"Very . . . very well," Amelia said as she got up.

"Did I wake you up a little too early?"

Amelia yawned and looked at the sky. "No . . . in fact, I have never been asleep for so long. In Arigog, we wake up before the sun rises."

"Really?"

"Yes, and we would get into a lot of trouble if we were to dare stay in bed a second longer." Amelia and Murean picked up a piece of fruit and began to eat. "This is my first time doing manual labor, so I must ask for your forgiveness if I do not do it as well as it must be done."

"I'm sure you'll understand what needs to be done after a few times."

"Although I should not be feeling this way, I am excited. I would always watch my maids do all of the work, and we would be in trouble if we were to attempt or pretend to do any form of chores."

After they ate their fruit, they left the slave tent and headed towards the water. Next to the flowing river was an enormous pile of filthy weapons and rags. "I already emptied the tents of their weapons, but I feel as if I forgot someone . . . let me think . . . Gremeak . . . . no, he has the most weapons . . . Montague . . . no, his weapons look the filthiest . . ." While Murean was thinking about whose tent she forgot to empty, Amelia gazed at the dirty weapons. Despite their lack of cleanliness, they could actually be useful . . . "If you're thinking that we could use them as a way to escape, don't bother. Gremeak is watching us to make sure that doesn't happen." Amelia turned around. Gremeak was standing next to the tent, staring at them.

"Why is he still here?"

"I don't know. He has a personal obsession about slaves and how they try to escape. The other hunters just don't care. As long as they could have someone other than themselves to get certain things done, it wouldn't bother them, even if all of the slaves disappeared. Let's just get this over with." Murean picked up a sword and rag, placed both into the water, and began to scrub off the filth. Amelia picked up a spear and did the same.

Although this was a usually unlikable form of cleaning labor, Amelia always wanted to do this, and now no one can tell her that she can't. Daleen does not ever again have to worry about Amelia doing her own job. Agatha is not here to tell her to stop or threaten to tell the Queen. Amelia does not even have to worry about her parents forcing her to stop this harmless act of kindness just to tell her that it's improper for a person like her to engage in such activities. As the thought came into her head, she smiled as the filth was taken away by the water. After a long time of cleaning, the pile of weapons was glistening as they were laid out to dry. When Amelia placed the last sword down, she turned around and nearly jumped. Gremeak was nowhere to be seen. Instead, Jack was standing nearby with an ugly look on his face.

Murean gasped. "Oh no, oh no, oh no. How could I forget him?" Her face turned pale as Jack began to walk towards them.

"What is wrong?" Amelia asked.

"His tent," Murean replied. "He's the one. I didn't empty any weapons from his tent."

Amelia's heart sank as Jack approached them. He first stared at Murean, who looked as if she was ready to faint. Then, he looked at Amelia as he went into his pocket and took out his dagger, protected in its case.

"I see you've cleaned everyone else's weapons except for mine."

"We're sorry," Murean replied. "We just finished the others . . . and we were just about to go into your tent and get . . ."

"Don't," he interrupted. He handed the dagger to Amelia and walked away.

"His only weapon is his dagger?"

"That's the only personal weapon he needs. And if he doesn't have that, he could kill with the weapons of his own enemies."

"I have a question."

"Sure, what is it?"

"Are there any male slaves?"

"Why are you asking?"

"Well, it is just that there are only female slaves here."

"Well, yes. There are male slaves all right. Long before you showed up, there were both males and females in the tent at that market. The last one was just sold a few days ago. Let's start cleaning the dagger so we can put the weapons away, and then we can go get some food."

"Allow me to do it." As she said this, Amelia began to remove it from the case.

"Gaaaugh!" Murean shouted in disgust.

The dagger was not only smeared with dirt, but with wet, maroon stains of blood. The blood of the slave salesman in the marketplace was still on the blade, and the same things were on the rag and in the case.

"I could have sworn that he cleaned this dagger," Amelia stared at the weapon, "I saw him."

"Then this blood must be from the case or something. It's not that much blood though, but it could still damage the weapon. You sure you don't want me to do it?"

"No. I am fine. It will only take a moment."

First, Amelia poured and emptied bloody water from the case. Murean decided to help anyway by taking the rag and scrubbing the stains off as much as possible. Then, Amelia took the bloody dagger and prepared to clean it. The second the blade touched the water, the filth was disappearing. Within seconds of being submerged, the dagger changed colors from brown to silver as maroon swirls danced in the rushing waters. With the rag, she scrubbed the rest of the filth off of the dagger underwater, from its silver blade to its leather wrapped hilt. When she had finished, the dagger was glistening in the noon sun.

Once the weapons had been oiled and dried, they separated and placed the weapons inside of the owners' tents. After placing all of the other weapons away, Amelia folded the rag and placed the dagger inside the case as she approached Jack's tent. Unlike the green hunters' tents, Jack's tent was blue with a fireplace outside. The inside was dark, but she saw what looked like a table. She slowly entered and placed the dagger and rag on the table. As she began to leave, she noticed a figure, slowly moving up and down . . .

"Boo!"

Amelia felt her heart jump as she turned around to face her attacker. Murean was right next to her with her hand over her mouth, trying her best not to laugh too loudly.

"Is it that funny?" asked Amelia as they left the tent.

"Yes," Murean replied, still giggling as she directed Amelia to a larger brown tent. Inside were slaves, rushing to cook food.

Edith looked up. "Oh, hello. We're making lunch. Come back in at sunset to serve dinner."

As she said this, she handed them plates of food. After lunch, Amelia and Murean went and washed a few clothes. Amelia handled the shirts and pants, and Murean handled the undergarments and armor. After the clothes dried in the setting sun, they folded up the clothes and placed them inside the tents. "Come on," Murean said. "We need to head to the kitchen tent."

They ran into the kitchen tent to find Edith and Anna rushing to cook meats over a fire and barrels of wine next to large empty cups.

"What took you so long?" Edith asked, "It's dinner time and this food needs to be served now."

"Sorry," Murean said, "we had to wash some clothes."

"Never mind that. Just hurry up and start serving. The hunters are getting impatient. Amelia, do you think you can handle doing a little serving, because it can be difficult. If need be, I can go and do it."

"No. I know that the food must be watched over by someone with experience and a good eye. I shall handle the serving."

"All right."

Amelia and Murean then took a few plates and left the tent.

Hands full of plates of hot food, Amelia struggled to keep up with Murean as they headed to the sound of laughter. Up ahead was a large tan tent that was the biggest in the whole camp and was the exact tent used at the market. Inside the tent were hunters, sitting together in front of three long, wooden tables, talking and laughing up a storm.

"Ah, there's the food," said a hunter.

Amelia and Murean quickly ran in and placed the food on the tables. Then they ran out, got more plates, and ran back into the dining tent. Amelia placed the food down and headed for the tent flap, but before she made it through, Edith and Anna met her with plates.

"Here," said Edith, handing Amelia her plates. "That way you won't have to run to the kitchen tent and back. I wish that they had never made us place the tents for the kitchen and dining area so far apart. It just doesn't make sense."

"Thank you." Amelia rushed back in and placed the plates down.

Within minutes, the tables were covered in plates of hot food, from loaves of golden-brown bread to delicious meats. After that, Amelia and Murean placed empty cups on the tables. Then, they left and returned with large pitchers of wine. One by one, they filled all of the cups with reddish-purple wine. As time passed, the hunters emptied their cups, and every time they did, Amelia and Murean had to fill the cups. One by one, the hunters began to get drunk, more drunk than Amelia had ever witnessed before in her life. Some were laughing uncontrollably to statements that weren't even close to being called a joke, some were singing to the heavens, and some looked a little green, as if they were extremely ill.

As more time progressed, Amelia noticed that Master Jack was not there. The man that had made her his slave was not here for dinner. When it seemed like all of the hunters were satisfied, Amelia and Murean left exhausted, arms carrying dirty plates and empty cups. When they entered the kitchen tent, Edith came out with food and a cup.

"Is that for you?"

"No, this is for Jack. I need you to deliver it to him for me."

"Of course." Amelia placed the dishes inside the kitchen tent and took the things out of Edith's arms.

"Just go and give this to him. Apparently, he's not feeling well. Oh, and don't just walk in. Let him know that you are there."

"Where is he?"

"He's in his tent."

With a fork and a hot plate of food in one hand and a cold cup of water in the other, Amelia walked towards Jack's tent. She got as close as she could to the tent flap, which was slightly ajar.

"Hello." There was no answer. "Is anyone there?" There was still no answer. "Master Jack, I have come to . . . to bring you your meal..."

"Come on in." Amelia nearly dropped the food when someone replied. With great caution, Amelia entered the tent, ready to run at any moment.

The inside was big and was lit by a few candles and from the fire outside, until the flap closed. On her left was Jack's bed, which was left unmade. On her right was a table with papers, maps, and the dagger, which was stabbed into the wood.

"I'm over here."

Amelia listened to the voice and followed it to the source. At the end of the tent was Jack standing next to another table, wide awake and, to Amelia's surprise, shirtless. His flat chest and muscular arms were glowing from the candlelight as he had just finished washing his face using the bowl of water next to him.

"Place it over here."

"Yes, sir." Amelia obeyed, placing the food, cup, and fork onto the table.

"Is that water?" he asked as he ate a forkful of food.

"Yes, sir."

"Have you fed the others?" he asked as he took a sip of water.

"Yes, sir. All of the hunters have received their meals."

"Good."

He began putting on a white shirt. Then, he went to the other table and picked up his dagger. All that Amelia could do was stand there with her head down as Jack walked towards her, twirling and doing slashing movements with his weapon. As Amelia kept her head down, an object appeared in front of her. Jack placed the dagger on her chin. Then, he slowly moved the blade, lifting her head until once again their eyes met. Despite the fact that there was a blade on her throat, Amelia enjoyed looking into his hazel eyes again. Jack then smiled, and Amelia, who was beginning to feel calm, slowly began to do the same . . .

"There you are, Jack!" Gremeak was shouting outside of the tent. He was so drunk that he could barely walk.

"Oh, hey," replied Jack, putting his dagger away.

"I thought I . . . *hic* . . . didn't see my best . . . *hic* . . . friend at the . . . at the . . ."

Before Gremeak could even finish his sentence, he ran out of sight. Amelia and Jack then heard Gremeak throwing up from a distance and then returning to the tent with his face turning green.

"Oh, dear," said Jack. "It looks like you drank too much again."

"Are you . . . *hic* . . . kidding me? This is how much I . . . *hic* . . . I usually drink. You know, . . . *hic* . . . you're my best friend, Jack. You'll always . . . *hic* . . . be my best friend."

"You look like you need to go to bed."

"Yeah, I . . . *hic* . . . I need to . . . *hic* . . . I need to go to bed."

Jack turned his head straight to Amelia. "Take him to his tent."

"Yes, sir." Amelia gave Jack one last look and walked out of the tent.

After she found Gremeak again, who was lying on the ground, she pulled and placed his arm on her shoulder and carried him away from Jack's tent. The entire time, Amelia struggled as Gremeak's overweight body was crushing her, and the combined smell of sweat, wine, and vomit filled her nostrils. When they made it to what she guessed was Gremeak's tent, she pushed him inside and headed straight to the slave tent. She opened it to find all of the slaves inside, most of whom were either sleeping or getting ready to sleep.

"Hello," Murean said as Amelia entered. "Your food is on your bed."

"Thank you," Amelia replied as she sat on her bed and began to eat the meal prepared for her. The food was cold, but delicious. In fact, this was some of the best food Amelia had ever tasted. "This is tremendous. Who made it?"

"What, the food? Edith made it." Amelia looked for Edith to thank her, but she was asleep in her bed. "Tonight was a long night, trying to serve all those hunters."

"I am in agreement," Amelia replied as she continued to eat her food. "That was an enormous feast."

Murean then let out a small laugh. "That was not a feast. That was their dinner. They eat like that every day."

"And what about their drinking? Surely they do not drink as much as they did tonight, do they?"

"They drink wine and beer as if they're fish underwater. They would drink to their heart's content, and then they wonder why they don't feel well, and then drink again." Amelia finished her plate as Murean went into her bed. "All right, I'm going to sleep." Murean then placed her head down and closed her eyes. Amelia placed the plate on the ground, promising herself to take it to the kitchen tent in the morning. She got up, walked to the tent flap, and closed it. She tied the string together, darkening the room. Then, she got in her bed, closed her eyes, and went to sleep.

Chapter 15:

The New Life

As days went by, Amelia was able to get used to her new life here in the Forest of Concealment. To make things easier for everyone, Anna divided the chores, aside from doing whatever the bounty hunters asked them to do. Amelia and Murean were to serve the meals, and Edith and Tama made the food. Everyone also had to clean the clothes and the insides of the tents. However, due to the fear of being killed, the slaves refused to go near Jack's tent, so this task was left to Anna. There was also a small cycle that was made. Every day, Amelia and Murean would serve a small breakfast, a small lunch, and an enormous dinner. Every dinner, the bounty hunters would stuff their faces with food and drink to the point that they could barely walk. And at each dinner, Master Jack would never show up to the dining tent, and Amelia would always have to give him his meals before heading off to bed. After a month since she was enslaved, Amelia was actually enjoying herself. She was away from the palace and all of the rules that she was forced to live by. She also enjoyed the new land and the company of the other slaves. She still, however, desired complete freedom and wanted to know how they were going to get out of here. Not to mention how she missed her maids and Mary and hoped that everything was all right.

That night, Amelia and Murean were heading to the kitchen tent to get the plates, but before Amelia entered, Murean stopped her. "Wait. I need to help you with your hair."

"I beg your pardon?"

"Your hair. I noticed that you struggle with it because it gets in the way. Here, turn around." Amelia obeyed, turning around. She could feel Murean combing through her hair with her fingers. Then, she braided it, took out a long strand of string, and tied the end. Within seconds, Amelia's hair was exactly like Murean's. "All done," she said. "Now it's not in the way, and if you need to take it out, just pull the string and comb through with your fingers."

"That is very kind of you, Murean. I am thankful for that."

"Come on. Let's serve the dinner." They went into the kitchen tent, took as many hot plates and empty cups as they could carry, and entered the dinning tent.

Within minutes, the bounty hunters received their food and wine. Amelia had just finished pouring a cup when she looked up and, to her surprise, Master Jack had entered and sat down.

"Jack!" shouted Gremeak, "I knew that some time or later you would join us." Jack did not say a word. He just smiled and stared at them as Amelia got him a hot plate of food and an empty cup. The second Amelia placed the things onto the table, Gremeak shouted, "Another round!"

Amelia obeyed and poured wine into his cup. "Another round!"

Amelia had barely finished pouring when Murean answered the order for another hunter. Before they knew it, all of the hunters were shouting for more wine so much that they even had to go get more pitchers. They poured cup after cup to the point that Amelia didn't even bother to look at their faces. As she reached for a cup and was ready to pour, a hand reached out and grabbed her. The tight grip made it impossible for Amelia to break free, let alone move her wrist. Master Jack, whose hand did not let go, just looked at her.

"No wine for me," he said after a moment of silence, "Just water." After he said that, he loosened his grip and let her go. Rubbing her wrist in pain, Amelia placed that pitcher down. Then, she grabbed a full pitcher, which contained water, and poured it into his cup. When she finished, she looked at Master Jack, who was staring back, smiling. Then, he placed his attention back on the other hunters. After Amelia placed the water pitcher down, she picked up the wine pitcher and waited to see if anyone wanted more wine.

"This is awful," Gremeak said, already sounding as if he'd drank too much. "This is just awful. I noticed our supply, and we'll be out of food soon. We're going to have to go and do a job. Maybe I could get paid to go and kill someone. They pay a good amount of money for that."

"Maybe this time I could help," said Lance.

"You? I'm not letting you take charge of anything. Not after last time when you..."

"Don't bring that up again! I keep telling you, it was not my fault!"

"I'm going to keep bringing it up until the day I die!"

146

"What exactly are you talking about?" asked a hunter.

"This poor excuse of a bounty hunter spent his first day ruining my job. He single-handedly lost me thousands of coins in one day. It was terrible, and at the same time hilarious."

"But," interrupted Lance, "most of you have probably heard it and would rather not hear it a second time."

"I'd like to hear it," said Jack.

"Very well," replied Gremeak. "I'm telling the story."

Suddenly, Amelia felt Murean tugging her arm. "I think I'm almost done serving," Murean whispered, "but it looks like they're finished with you. You could leave if you want, and I could meet you back at the slave tent."

"No, wait," Amelia replied. "I wish to hear this."

"Fine." Murean walked away as Amelia walked near Gremeak.

"You see, Jack," Gremeak started, "the cage that you're using is the second best cage that I've ever bought. The first one that I bought was a year ago. The cage was smaller, but tougher. Like your cage, it was pulled by a horse and made of the finest metal. I bought the cage and caught a slave a few days later on a windy day. At this time, it was Lance's first time being a hunter, and I had brought him along with me." Lance looked the other way, giving a nasty scowl. "I had stupidly asked him to lock the door and hold the key, which he happily accepted with no delay."

Amelia had managed to find an empty chair and, against her fears, sat next to Master Jack, eagerly listening to the story. "I went on and had a conversation with a few other hunters that were with us when I heard him coming around, saying the girl was crying and begging."

"She was," Lance said. "She grabbed me by my clothes and shook me, begging me to let her out." As he said that, he held his fists in front of him and moved them to and fro, as if shaking someone.

"Anyway, we were talking for a while, and then we were getting ready to get on when suddenly . . . there was an enormous creaking sound . . . the entire cage was leaning!"

"What?" asked a hunter. "How did it lean?"

"Foolish Lance had managed to place the cage right near a large cliff, and it was beginning to move. He said that placing it there would keep the slave from trying to leave."

Amelia sat on the edge of her seat in excitement. Most of the stories that she had heard had moral endings that had to deal with being proper and doing as one was told, but this one sounded otherwise.

"The horse immediately started to panic, and it began kicking the cage!"

"No," said Jack.

"Yes," replied Gremeak, "and he was kicking really well, too. Within seconds, he kicked pieces off and got himself free. Here's my proof."

He reached into his pocket and tossed onto the table a crooked and rusty piece of metal. "This used to be a straight lock and was the strongest part that connected the horse to the cage. The horse had managed to kick the entire thing off!"

Sounds of astonishment filled the air as everyone looked at the broken piece.

"So the horse was actually able to free himself?" asked a hunter.

"Yes, but it was already too late. By the time he was able to free himself, the cage had already fallen off the cliff, *and* because of its weight and lack of balance, the horse fell with it! I immediately asked Lance what happened, and he told me that he didn't know because he used an object to stop the cage from moving. And you will not believe what object he was referring to so he could keep the cage still."

"What?"

"A branch!"

"What?"

"Yes, he used a branch to hold, and, as you may not have known, it broke!"

"So then what happened?" asked Master Jack.

"The cage and the horse fell off the cliff and into the water below. At first, I'm furious at this, and then he tells me that he lost the key, too."

"I did," said Lance. "I didn't know what happened to the key. I wore it as a necklace and I had it, and the next thing I knew, it was gone."

"Likely story," said another hunter as the room filled with laughter.

"So anyway," Gremeak said, "I'm watching the cage go down into the water, and then . . . the slave popped up to the surface! Yes! Somehow, the door was unlocked, the slave broke free, and she came up to the surface! *And* the horse came up to the surface a second later!" An enormous roar of laughter filled the dining tent.

"So then what happened?" asked a hunter.

"The slave and horse got on land, the slave got onto the horse, and they rode away! They left as if they were in a story, riding off into a sunset. It was pathetic!"

For what felt like several minutes, the hunters struggled to stop laughing, then, Gremeak shouted, "Another round!"

Amelia quickly got up and helped Murean pour the cups.

Several more minutes later, the hunters were drunk to the point that they started singing a song:

"From the rising dawn with color of red,
to the sky with shades of blue!
That hugs the yellow sun and the green grass,
which grows with me and you!
No matter how many years will pass,
there's one thing we have known.
No matter where we go in life
it will always be our home!
It's always our hooooommmmeee!"

Cheers were shouted as Amelia bent down to pour Gremeak's cup as he shouted, "Another round!" Suddenly, an object flew into the room, brushing right under Amelia's nose as it zoomed inside.

"Aargh!"

Amelia turned her head to the source of the sound. Murean was standing still next to a pole with a purple arrow through her hair.

Everyone stood up in silence as she stood still, unable to break free.

"Aargh! Help!"

"Murean!"

Amelia placed the pitcher down and ran to help her friend. Remembering what Murean instructed before dinner, Amelia pulled the string and combed through, letting a brown cascade of hair fall down Murean's back. She then moved her out of the way, freeing her from the arrow, which had pierced the pole. They backed up as hunters gathered near the pole. Master Jack, who walked the closest to it, reached out, removed the arrow, and examined it.

"The arrow with feathers of purple," said Gremeak.

"Destramechs," said Master Jack. All of the hunters began to turn pale as they uttered words of fear under their breaths.

"Does it have a symbol carved on it?"

"Yes, a mountain. They're coming to conquer."

"What are we going to do?"

Master Jack did not reply immediately. He looked down, holding the arrow, and then looked up.

"Men, sharpen your weapons and prepare for a battle!" Everyone, including Amelia and Murean, scrambled out of the dining tent. The hunters ran into their tents and came out with their clean weapons. They then sat on the ground and began to sharpen them. "Slaves," called Master Jack, "Find us some rocks and . . . never mind. Find all the other slaves, go in your tent, and stay there. If I see one slave tonight, there will be a problem."

"Yes, sir," answered Amelia. Then, she and Murean ran as fast as they could to the kitchen tent.

"Master Jack has just given us a new command," said Amelia as they entered. "We need to go to the slave tent . . . now!"

"Amelia, calm down," Edith said. "Murean, what's happening?"

"We don't have time to explain right now," said Murean as she began to pick up food and place it into a nearby basket. "Just get some food and head to the slave tent. Hurry!"

Edith and Tama obeyed, gathering whatever food they could find at the moment and putting it in the basket. They then hurried and followed the other slaves into the slave tent.

"Is everyone here?" Amelia asked as she entered.

"Almost," replied Tama. "We just need to wait for Anna."

Amelia then sat and looked around. Mila was sitting on her bed by herself, clutching her doll and shaking as people zoomed past her. Murean, who still looked horror stricken, just went over and sat on her bed, rubbing the spot in her hair where the arrow struck. Everyone in the tent looked worried except for Delilah, who was sitting on her bed as if absolutely nothing was wrong.

After a few minutes, Anna entered with sweat on her head. "Does someone want to tell me what's going on here? The hunters are sending us to our tent early, and they all look as if they've seen a ghost."

"A purple arrow was shot during dinner. It almost killed me and Murean."

"An arrow with feathers of purple?"

"Yes."

"Destramechs."

Almost instantly, Delilah got up and, without saying a word, left the tent.

"She does realize that she will receive high consequences from Master Jack for leaving the tent, doesn't she?"

"I guess."

"So, why does it seem as if Destramechs are very dangerous?"

"The Destramechs, unlike the ones told to you, are more than just improper. They are dangerous and relentless warriors. They're highly skilled, and they will stop at nothing to get what they want. The arrow, Destramechs use arrows as their way of communication in new lands. Did it have some kind of marking on it? It would tell us what they want."

"Yes. The arrow had a mountain on it."

"It represents land. They've come to conquer."

"But why here?" asked Murean. "Why try to conquer the Forest of Concealment?"

"I don't know. They've been expanding their land for years. They might even know that there are bounty hunters here."

"Then this is good. If they kill the hunters, we shall be free."

"No, it's not good," said Tama. "If they kill the hunters, we will be their slaves."

"And what do they do with their slaves?"

"Pure torture. They torture their slaves all day and night. Sometimes, they do it to get information, but they mostly do it just for the fun of it. For instance, they're known to tie your limbs to horses and rip you apart."

"They also could tie you to a tree and throw weapons at you for target practice," said Anna.

"But if you're lucky," said Murean, "you could either find a way to be free or be killed during the raids."

"How long do you think we will have to wait here until an attack?"

"I'm not sure," said Anna. "It varies. Years ago, they sent the arrow with a mountain mark to a large village. They later managed to cut off supplies of food and blocked the roads with ambushes. The entire village suffered for three months. It then went to the point that one day they were driven to insanity and just killed each other. By the time the Destramechs actually attacked, the land was burning and covered in dead bodies. The only ones who survived it were four girls who made some trouble and were hiding from their parents to avoid a good scolding."

After a moment of silence, a thought came into Amelia's head. "Murean."

"Hmm."

"Why did you not like the story? The one Master Gremeak told at dinner. Why did you not enjoy it?"

"Well, it's not that I didn't enjoy it. The story is a little old."

"So you have heard it before?"

"Not exactly. I didn't hear it, I was there. I was the slave who escaped."

"What?" Almost everyone said this in unison.

"Yes," she said with a sigh. "That was me, but you don't have to get too excited over it. It's not like I'm the first one to escape Gremeak."

"True," said Anna, "but your escape seems to be the only one he talks about."

"Could you tell us your side of the story?" Amelia asked. "After all, we do not have anything else to do."

"I guess I could, but I'm only telling it once."

Everyone then got up, went to the basket, sat back down with some food, and began to eat as Murean cleared her throat. "Like Gremeak said, it was a year ago on a cool, windy day. I don't remember how, but one way or another, I was captured again." Amelia took a bite of a green apple as she sat down, eager to hear the story.

"They threw me in the cage, which for some reason was near a cliff. Lance came to look at me, probably to look at his first prisoner. Anyway, he was wearing the key as a necklace. I pretended to act like a desperate girl and grabbed his clothes and cried for mercy." As she said that, she took a bite of her bread, placed it down, held two fists in the air and shook them rapidly. "While shaking him, I had managed to grab the key and snap it off of his neck. If he had given a second glance at me as he walked away, he would have noticed the strap of the necklace coming out of my fists."

"But what about the cage falling?" interrupted Mila.

"That was something that I didn't plan on happening."

"What do you mean?"

"My plan was to wait until we were moving. That way, I could get out without the hunters noticing. I was walking around waiting for them to move when I heard a cracking sound. I don't know if it was a branch or not, but whatever it was, it was failing. I quickly went toward one of the walls with bars and held on for dear life. I could hear the object break and the horse panicking as the cage started moving in the opposite direction. Before I knew it, I was falling and plummeting into the water. Luckily, the cage was strong and it was able to stop the impact from harming me." She then took another bite of her bread. "I quickly unlocked the cell and swam to the surface. Coincidentally, the horse came up to the surface right next to me. I pulled the horse to land, I got onto the horse, and rode off."

Sounds of amazement filled the tent as Murean took another bite of her bread.

"Yes. I used to hate the fact that my mom made me learn how to ride a horse, but after that day, I'm grateful that she did."

Chapter 16:

The Dreadful Arrival

The sun had set in the sky. It had been ten days since the arrow was shot into the dining tent. The hunters kept themselves alert, avoiding drinking and barely eating. The slaves were also being affected, as they were not told to do much. The hunters didn't make much of a mess in their tents, so there was nothing to clean, and since they were eating little, there was not much to serve. The only important order that was given was to just stay in the slave tent. Everyone already knew that the Destramechs were here, as they could see the smoke from the fire of their nearby camp.

Amelia was on her bed playing with Mila's hair.

"What exactly do you suppose the hunters plan to do?" she asked Murean, who was sitting on her bed.

"I don't know. The hunters have been doing nothing but watching things for days. I don't think they have even made a plan yet."

"I also heard that our food supply is starting to go down, but how are the Destramechs surviving without food after ten days?"

"They're probably getting supplies straight from Destera."

"Do you think that this will end soon?"

"Only time will tell."

As time continued, the land did not seem as bright as before. The hunters gradually began to stay in their tents to the point that the slaves had to serve them all individually. After two months passed, Amelia served the last hunter his lunch and exited into the snowy outdoors. Dark clouds were combining in the sky as snow began to fall. Cold wind blew in Amelia's face as she ran into the slave tent. A few slaves were inside, trying their best to fight the cold. Tama looked up and saw her. Then, she went towards her and handed her a blanket.

"Here you go. It's clean, and none of the hunters claimed it as theirs."

Amelia took the blanket and warmed herself up. Hours passed as they all sat in the cold tent, doing their best to stay warm. "Do we have an idea on how to get out of here yet?

Perhaps we should leave now, while the hunters are distracted with the pending attack."

"I was thinking about that for a while," said Anna. "Unfortunately, there are a few problems with that. The hunters have been keeping a sharp eye on everything. If we were to try to leave now, they might confuse us for Destramechs and attack us. Plus, we're in the Forest of Concealment. We would have no way of knowing directions and would go in circles. We might even end up walking right into the Destramech camp. Now, Tama and I have been thinking over a new idea. I say we wait until after the battle to escape."

"The problem is," Tama said, "we don't know when they will attack or the outcome."

"But, if the hunters win, the Destramechs would be gone. Then, the hunters would be so busy celebrating that we could find a map and all of us could sneak out of here."

"I knew it," someone snapped, "I knew it! I just knew it!" Delilah ran into the tent with her face red in anger and her body shivering from the cold. "I should have known from the beginning. You all were planning to escape."

Amelia was confused for a minute, and then remembered how when they arrived here, Anna tricked

Delilah into thinking that they were done with their desires of leaving.

"Oh," Anna said sarcastically, "sorry. You weren't supposed to know."

"After all that I have told you, after all that I have warned you of, you . . . you still allow yourselves to be consumed by your . . . your prideful arrogance in your desires to betray our master?"

"If it means that we can earn our freedom, yes."

"We are to be loyal. Listen to me. We must be loyal like me, like a Destrame..."

"You," Tama interrupted, "it's all so clear now."

"What?"

"You're the reason they're here. You're the reason why we have been surrounded for months. Because you're a stupid Destramech!"

"How dare you!"

"Think about it. Everything was fine until you were here, talking about your 'loyalty'. Now all of a sudden an army of Destramechs is trying to take over this land. And since you are the only Destramech here, the rest of us are going to die. Can't you see? It's your entire fault!"

"I have nothing to do with the Destramech army! For I have been a loyal slave for nine years! I have absolutely no idea why the Destramechs are here, *nor* will I concern myself about it!"

"So," Amelia calmly interrupted, "you are saying that you being here and the Destramechs being here is all a coincidence?"

"Yes!"

"I'm not believing it," said Tama.

"Well it doesn't matter why they are really here," said Anna. "The main fact is that we can escape, if we can, after the battle. Delilah, whether we win or lose, you can go with the Destramechs. You can go home and we will be free."

"I believe that that is a swell idea," Amelia said happily. "What shall you say, Delilah?"

Delilah didn't answer. She just stood there with a look of doubt, confusion, and fear. But before she could say anything, Edith entered out of breath.

"Edith," said Murean, "what's wrong?"

"We are all needed in the dining tent."

"What?"

"Yes. Master Jack is talking to all of the hunters, and he wants all of us there to serve dinner."

"But why all of us? Amelia and I have been doing it for months."

"I don't know. They just want all of us there."

"All right."

The slaves went and entered the kitchen tent. They were handed hot plates of food as they headed to the dining tent. As they were about to enter, Lance opened it with a stern look on his face. Inside, the hunters looked hungry, and they weren't as merry as usual. As Amelia served the food, she noticed that the hunters were wearing pale looks on their faces and shiny pieces of armor, except for Master Jack, who was wearing no armor at all. The tables, along with the plates and cups, were covered with shiny weapons, from Gremeak's sword to Montague's mace. Several minutes were spent in silence. Most of the hunters were either eating like Lance, who was taking small bites, or like Gremeak, who was wolfing down his entire plate.

After a while, Jack placed his fork down and loudly cleared his throat. "I'll make this quick. As you all know, the Destramechs have been here for several months. They have surrounded us and possibly cut off our only safe way out."

"Well, can't we leave by some other route?" asked a hunter.

"No, unless you have a map of the forest, because right now I don't have one." A few hunters chuckled as the man lowered his head in embarrassment. "Now," Jack continued, "If we let them keep us surrounded any longer, we will die in this forest, and for some of us that might be a high chance. But I have one thing to say about this: if I die here, I'm going to die fighting and killing every one of those Destramechs I can get my hands on. I just want to know if you all are willing to do the same."

"Of course, Jack," said another hunter, "Those Destramechs aren't going to stop until this land is conquered, so we won't stop until they are defeated or until we take our last breaths!" An uproar of cheers followed the man's words.

"All right. I doubt that this will ever happen, but I feel as if I need to say it. Gremeak, if something happens to me and you survive, you will have all of my stuff. My tents, my dagger, my riches, and my slaves . . . all of this would belong to you."

"Why, thank you." replied Gremeak, who had just finished a mouthful of bread.

"Now that we have that taken care of, let me talk about the main matter. I asked you all to come armored and with your weapons for a reason. I refuse to be trapped here like a caged animal any longer. We are going to attack. Everyone all right with this?" The hunters either uttered a confident "yes" or nodded their heads in agreement. "Then it's settled. So prepare yourselves. We will leave and attack before dawn."

"Ummmm . . . Jack?" said Lance.

"What?"

"We might not have to wait until dawn to attack."

The whole tent went quiet. Then, a small sound of marching filled the air. Amelia, who was filling a cup with water, placed the pitcher on a table and went to take a look outside. Emerging from the trees was an army walking into the camp, paying no regard to the objects that they stepped on in their path.

"It's the Destramechs! Prepare to fight!" shouted Gremeak as he stood up and raised his sword.

"No," said Jack, "hide your weapons. Let's make it seem as if we're defenseless."

Everyone began putting their weapons away or hiding it under the table. Amelia and Lance got out of the way as Jack quickly placed his dagger into his pocket. Suddenly, two different hands entered the tent and pulled the flap wide opened. An army in rows of four entered the tent. They were dressed in purple and silver armor as they came inside and stood right in the middle of the room. To Amelia, the men were standing there so perfectly that even their blinking seemed to be in unison. Then, two men entered and stood in front of the army. They too were dressed in purple and silver armor, along with purple capes, and one of them wore a purple phoenix on his chest. Amelia could not believe it. After all these years of being told what the Destramechs are, now she meets a small army of them face-to-face. Everyone stared at the new uninvited guests with pale looks on their faces except for Jack, who still looked calm. "Well, hello, gentlemen," he said after a moment of silence. "Lovely night, isn't it?" No one replied right away, only giving expressionless looks as they stared at what seemed like pure emptiness. Then, the knight with the purple phoenix stepped forward with a stern look on his face.

"I," the man announced loudly, "am Sir Borin Banter, leader of the Violet troops. We are Destramechs."

"Hello, Sir Banter. I am Jack..."

"We are well aware of who you are. Jack Vernono, peasant of the land of Merrigan, deadliest bounty hunter that has ever lived. Yes, you have killed hundreds of people, including other bounty hunters and Destramechs, yet you have managed to receive this accomplishment at the surprisingly young age of twenty-two. One of your accomplishments includes setting a Destramech camp on fire using only one burning arrow."

"Oh, I remember tha..."

"As you may not be intelligent enough to be aware of, an arrow was shot into this tent months ago."

"I know," replied Jack, now getting irritated. "It nearly killed two of my slaves."

"The arrow," said Sir Banter, completely disregarding Jack's statement, "was marked with a mountain. We have come to conquer."

"I know what it said, but before we do anything else, can I at least ask you something?"

You . . . you may," Banter replied with a bit of hesitation and regret.

"You Destramechs have been expanding to mainly cities and villages. Why do you want to take over the middle of a forest that no one else enters?"

"We are not really here to conquer the land . . . we are here to conquer you."

"Conquer me?"

"Yes. You and your fellow bounty hunters have harmed our lands for too long. We are here to arrest you and allow you to make your choices."

Jack did not say a word, but sat there in silence, looking at his men, his slaves, and then his plate. He then ate a forkful and lifted the plate. "Gremeak, put this over there on that table please."

"Umm . . . sure Jack. No problem." Gremeak took the plate and fork, and one-by-one, the hunters placed the dishes on the other table.

"Now," said Jack as he took a sip of water and directed Amelia to place the cup and Gremeak's plate onto the other table. "What choices are you talking about?"

"You, Jack Vernono, are the best bounty hunter these lands have ever known. You are gifted with the skills that we need. You have the choice of being taken to train our men."

"To spend years doing it?"

"No. Unfortunately, you would know too much about our weaknesses and we would have to execute you."

Jack took two hunters' plates and gave them to Murean and Edith. "What is my other option?"

"Your other option is to not do it and instead be held in jail and executed for your crimes."

Jack had just cleared the table when Banter finished. "So, you are saying that I could train your men or rot in a cold cell. But either way, you plan to execute me."

"Yes, but it is your choice, which you can make when we arrive at our destination. Now, if you would stand up, we will be taking you to Destera."

"And what makes you think that I would actually come willingly?"

Banter was left speechless, not actually expecting that response. "Wha-what do you mean?"

"I mean do you honestly think that I'm going to let you come into my camp, arrest me and my fellow hunters, take my stuff and slaves, take me to Destera, make me either train your men or rot in a cell and then get executed?"

"You will if you value your life. After all, what shall you try to do, fight us? We outnumber you."

"Are you sure, because it looks as if we are equal in numbers. And as you may not be intelligent enough to be aware of, you are surrounded by the best hunters in the land and you have to deal with me. We are not outnumbered, but you are without a doubt outmatched. If I am going to die, I'm going to do it while trying to strike you down!"

"Is that so? Well, I tried to be reasonable with you, but if this is how you want it, then so be it."

There was a long moment of silence. Then before Amelia could notice, Banter pulled out four large knives. Jack quickly stood up, flipped the table, and ducked as Banter threw the knives. The first knife went through the tent where Jack's head was. The second and third knives went through the tent where Jack's chest and stomach were. The fourth knife went through the table, nearly inches away from touching his face. Then, without delay, Jack quickly stood up and took out his dagger.

"Now!"

All at once, the hunters stood up and showed their weapons. The Destramechs, who weren't expecting their weapons, stood there with their eyes widened.

"Men," shouted Banter, "remember: We know no fear. For we are Destramechs! Attack!" As he said that, he pulled out his sword and raised it in the air. The men, coming back to their senses, took out their swords and charged in all directions.

Chapter 17:

The Battle That No One Expected

War screams filled the air as the hunters and Destramechs fought. Banter was heading straight for Jack, but two hunters distracted him. The caped soldier that was next to Banter charged at Jack, barely missing his chest with every slash. As two more Destramechs joined in, the caped soldier had managed to knock Jack's dagger out of his hands. Looking down at the table, Jack used his foot and quickly broke off one of the wooden legs. With his new weapon in hand, he hit the first soldier on his legs, knocking him down. He then swung and hit the second soldier so hard that Amelia heard his neck snap and watched him drop dead. The caped soldier then charged, but Jack was able to strike him in the head, causing him to drop and his head to bleed. As Jack picked up his dagger, the first soldier he struck was getting up. Before the soldier could strike, Jack launched forward and stabbed him right in the chest.

Then, he took out the dagger and snatched his sword as the soldier dropped dead, and left the tent. Banter had just killed his opponents when he looked for Jack and instead saw the caped soldier on the ground. He stood there for a moment as his face began to turn scarlet. "Jaaaack!" he yelled, "your head is mine!" And with that, he ran out of the tent.

As most of the fighting was now occurring outside, Amelia and the others opened the tent to look. Gremeak was now holding two swords as he struck his opponents down. Lance was fighting a Destramech, but it looked as if the enemy was winning. Nearby, a group of soldiers was backing away from Montague, who had just broken a soldier's neck with his bare hands. Suddenly, a hunter, who still happened to be inside, grabbed Murean by her wrist and pulled her out of the tent. Amelia and Anna quickly grabbed her arm.

"What are you doing?" asked Murean as Amelia and Anna started to pull her back.

"These hunters aren't going to last a second against these Destramechs. I'm leaving, and you're coming with me."

"Let me go!"

"Aarrugh!"

Flaming arrows struck the hunter in the back and neck, causing him to release Murean as he fell dead and caught fire.

"Well," said Amelia as they ran out of the tent, "at least a cremation may not have to be in order."

As she said that, she heard a loud scream. Delilah was backing up towards a burning tent as Destramechs surrounded her, ready to kill.

"Delilah," Anna shouted, "the necklace! Show them your necklace!"

Delilah quickly obeyed, pulling out her necklace. The eyes of the Destramechs widened as they lowered their swords and stared at Delilah's purple phoenix. They then ran away, leaving Delilah standing there, not knowing what to do.

"Go, Delilah," shouted Amelia. "Go!"

Delilah obeyed, running after the Destramechs and disappearing behind a burning tent.

"We should go to the slave tent," said Edith.

"Better than being out here," replied Anna.

They all ran as fast as they could, avoiding fires, swords, and flying arrows. When they finally got to the slave tent, they ran inside. Edith was the last to come in, standing there out of breath.

"That was clo—"

Swoosh! Swoosh! Swoosh!

Everyone turned around as burning arrows were shot behind them and the tent caught fire.

"Run!" Everyone hurried out of the tent as the fire began to grow.

"Is everyone all right?" Amelia asked.

Murean looked up. "I thin—"

"Mila!"

Amelia turned around to the source of the voice and, to her horror, saw the glimpse of a small girl running back inside the burning slave tent. Anna quickly ran inside and came back out with Mila, who was now clutching her doll.

"Have you lost your mind?" yelled Anna. "You could have died!"

"I had to get the doll. I had to!"

Anna then let go of Mila and stared at a dead soldier with a sword in his back. Anna then reached out, took the sword, and picked up his shield.

"What are you doing?" asked Murean.

"Raising our chances. If we fight, we can help the hunters win."

"I like that idea," said Tama as she grabbed a dead hunter's battle axe and shield.

"But some of us may not know how to fight," said Amelia.

"Then stay hidden."

Anna and Tama began to run toward the battle, knocking down two soldiers in their path. Meanwhile, the others dodged burning patches of grass and ran into the kitchen tent.

"Let's just try to stay here until it's over," said Edith.

Amelia, curious about what was happening, took a peek outside. There were small glimpses of things that were happening. Anna was striking a soldier, Gremeak was just knocked down, and Lance was nowhere to be found. Amelia then looked and saw Jack and Banter near the forest. Jack, who was now holding a sword, had just knocked Banter down. Then, they both stopped moving. Amelia looked closely and realized that an arrow was stabbed into Jack's clothes, trapping him to a tree.

"Master Jack is stuck," she cried. "He is in need of help!" Amelia ran out of the tent, but Murean grabbed her.

"Are you mad?" said Edith. "You'll die before you could get to him."

"If he dies, we will belong to Gremeak!"

And with that, she loosened Murean's grip and ran. She went past flying arrows and the slave tent, which was now in flames.

"Amelia," cried Anna, "where are you going?"

But Amelia didn't answer. She went past hunters and Destramechs, nearly getting caught in their sword fight. She went past Banter, who was unconscious and his face was tear dried, and ran straight to Jack.

"I'm stuck," he said. "I can't get out." Amelia tried to help, but with the arrow stuck in the bark, Amelia and Jack struggled to break free. Suddenly, Amelia heard a loud war cry. A large Destramech was charging towards them, causing both hunters and Destramechs to run out of his way. The arrow was becoming more and more loose, but Amelia feared that the soldier would kill them before the arrow would be free. As they continued to struggle, Jack looked down. "Spear!"

"Pardon?"

"Spear! Get the spear! I'll try to snap the arrow!"

Amelia looked down and saw a large spear that was pierced into the dirt. With the soldier getting closer, Amelia quickly ran and grabbed the spear. "You must be joking!" The spear was just as stuck as the arrow.

"Hurry," cried Jack, "He's getting closer!"

"I am trying!"

With every second the spear was becoming loose the soldier would get a step closer, making it seem as if her fate was imminent. Then, Amelia felt the spear becoming free and she lifted the dirt-covered weapon from the ground. As soon as she did, the soldier ran right through it. Amelia let go of the spear and backed away as she could hear Jack breaking the arrow behind her. The soldier, not uttering a sound, reached out and pulled the bloody spear out of his stomach. He then looked at Amelia, showed her his bloody teeth and lunged forward. But before Amelia could realize it, Jack grabbed her and threw her to the ground. Then, he lifted up a sword and ran it through the soldier's chest, letting it go as the soldier fell dead. As Amelia got herself up, Banter was regaining consciousness and looked straight at the dead soldier. His eyes widened and mouth opened as he got up, staring at the new corpse. Other Destramechs began to notice the body and ran towards the forest. Banter, who was still bewildered, turned around and did the same.

"Oh, no you don't," shouted Gremeak. "You Destramechs aren't going to escape us that easily. Men, attack!"

War cries were shouted as he and other hunters chased the Destramechs. Jack watched the hunters run, but he looked too tired to join them. Instead, he walked away in the opposite direction, and Amelia followed. They kept walking until Jack stopped in front of two Destramechs piled on top of each other. He picked up one Destramech, threw him aside, and flipped the other one over. The Destramech he flipped over was dead with his eyes wide opened and Jack's dagger in his chest. With both hands gripping the handle and his boot on his chest, Jack was able to remove the dagger. Then, they walked toward the river and he placed the weapon into the water.

"Slave."

"Yes, sir?"

"It looks as if the battle is over. Go on and clean up the mess."

"And what should we do with the bodies, sir?"

"Pile them up and burn them."

"Yes, sir."

Amelia then turned around and walked away as Jack continued to clean his dagger.

Chapter 18:

Aftermath

With caution, Amelia walked towards the kitchen tent. "Oh, my goodness," said Murean as she came out and hugged her. "Are you all right? You could've died out there."

"I am fine. Is everyone else all right?"

"Well, yes. Anna got hurt, but we're all fine." Amelia and Murean entered the tent.

Inside, most of the slaves were surrounding Anna, who was holding a damp cloth next to her side. Tama was sitting on a pot next to her with a worried look on her face.

"Anna," said Amelia, "how are you feeling?"

"As if I was cut with a sword," Anna replied with a chuckle. "I'm fine. I just got hurt a little, and the strangest thing is that I don't even know who struck me."

Amelia then looked over and, to her disbelief, saw Delilah standing in a corner with her usual high elegance look. "I thought that you went with the Destramechs. I thought that you were going home."

Delilah looked at her and softly said, "A true Destramech is loyal. If I was to escape and return to Destera, my people would have me judged and severely punished me for disloyalty. Believe me when I say that I am better off staying here."

"Did we win?" asked Anna.

"Yes," said Amelia, "as of now, we are victorious."

"Good. It felt great to fight, even though I got hurt, but I know that I was better than Lance. Last time I saw him, he was being chased by Destramechs." Everyone laughed at the thought of Lance running for his life with a high-pitched squeal. "So," said Anna after the laughter died, "I heard that you went to save Jack. Is he all right?"

"Yes, Master Jack is alive."

"Good."

"And he wishes for us to clean the mess and burn the dead."

"Oh, lovely," said Murean. Everyone except Anna stood up and walked out of the tent. After a few seconds, Anna attempted to do the same.

"Oh, no. Not you, Anna," said Edith, "We need you to stay here and rest."

"Fine." And with that, Anna went and sat back down.

Murean and Edith took large pots, filled them with water, and put out the fires. The once big slave tent was gone, and the beds were too fragile for anyone to even sit on. After they put out the fires, they all went to collect the bodies. Amelia struggled to hold her stomach as she dragged heavy, bloody, ice-cold corpses. "Awww," said Murean as she dragged the burnt hunter that tried to take her earlier. "I remember him now. He was one of the hunters that was there when I escaped in the cage. What a shame." She then happily tossed him into the pile. After a few hours, the fires had been put out, the ripped tents were fixed, and the bodies were piled up and ready to be burned.

"There. Do you know how to start a fire?" Amelia asked Edith.

"Yes. I..."

"Slaves," called Jack, "how is the camp?"

"All has been cleaned up, sir."

"And the bodies?"

"The bodies have been piled up and are ready to be burned, sir," said Edith.

"Good. Go on an..."

"Jack!"

Everyone looked. Gremeak and the hunters emerged from the forest. Each hunter was either carrying or pulling something. Some of them were carrying food, clothes, and wood. Others were pulling small wagons and holding heavy objects. "Gremeak!" shouted Jack as he walked towards them. As the slaves joined him, Amelia noticed something. While the hunters were holding stuff, Gremeak was holding his sword in one hand and his side with the other.

"Is . . . is he hurt?"

"What?" asked Tama.

"Gremeak. I think . . . I think he is hurt." They quickly hurried to the hunters to get a better look.

"We did it!" shouted Gremeak. "We defeated the Destramechs and we looted their entire camp! They had enough supplies to keep a whole village satisfied for months!"

"Gremeak," said Jack as he stopped, "you're holding your side. Are you wounded?"

"I bet you a whole lot of people would wish that that was happening, but no. I ate too much before the battle, and my side hurts a little. But you should have been there, Jack. The fight was glorious. I can't say the same for Lance. I had to take down the Destramechs that were chasing him."

"For the last time, I had it under control."

"So," said Jack "what did you all find at the camp that's enough for a village?"

"We found food, clothes, even tents. Surprisingly, only one of them is purple. That one probably belongs to that Banter. Plus, we saw several men run away. They might have been slaves, but even if they weren't, they would've probably made good ones."

"Any Destramech escape?"

"Yes. A whole bunch of them, but they won't last long."

"What does he mean they will not last long?" Amelia asked.

"Well," said Edith, "if a Destramech army goes into battle and retreats, their actions are seen as a sign of failure, and they're executed as punishment. They won't kill the leader though. Not a leader like Banter. They need his skills, so they will probably keep him alive."

"Did you find any papers?" asked Jack.

"Papers?"

"Yes, papers. Any maps, a list, a plan of attack, a reason as to how they were able to find us."

"Nope. None of tha... you!" Amelia turned around and saw Delilah approaching them. "I saw you running off. You thought that you could just esca- wha- wha-where did you get that?" He was pointing straight at Delilah's necklace.

"What do you mean?"

"Where did you get it? Who did you steal that from?"

"I did not steal this. This is mine. I have had this necklace all of my life."

"You're lying."

"No, please. I speak the truth. I am a Destramech."

"A . . . a . . . a Destramech?"

"Yes."

After a moment of silence, Jack said, "Get in your tent, now."

"But it was burned down, sir" said Amelia. "We do not have a tent or beds."

"Here," said Gremeak, handing her parts of a yellow tent wrapped up in a bundle. "I could have the men get you some beds. We now have plenty of those."

"Good," said Jack, "make the tent and stay there."

Immediately, Amelia and the others left for the kitchen tent and brought Anna to the spot. They removed what was left of the tent and beds and replaced them. The new slave tent was much bigger and warmer than the last one, and the new beds were bigger and more comfortable.

"I guess we should go to bed," said Murean.

"I wouldn't bother," said Anna, "the sun will be rising in a few hours."

"Well, at least there is peace," said Delilah.

"There would have already been peace," said Tama, "if it weren't for you Destrame—"

"Enough, Tama!" snapped Edith.

"But she's a Destrame—"

"We all know that she is from Destera, but that doesn't mean that you have to ridicule her because of it."

"Why does this matter to you?"

"Because not all Destramechs are bad!"

Everyone stood in shock. "What do you mean, Edith," asked Amelia.

Edith walked over, sat on her new bed, and took a deep breath. "When I was young," she began, "my grandmother, Matilda, would tell me and my sister stories for years before she died. She told us that there was once a time where the

Arigogians and the Destramechs were the closest of friends."

"Friends?" asked Mila.

"Yes. Long before the Great War, the people of Arigog and Destera were the closest of people, almost like lovable siblings. When my grandmother was little, she and the family lived outside of the towns next to a family of happy Destramechs. The family's daughter was my grandmother's best friend. There was also a lot of helpfulness in the land, but the people would help each other the most. If an Arigogian was in trouble, a Destramech would help them, and if a Destramech was in peril, an Arigogian would come to their rescue. The lands were truly inseparable."

"What happened?" asked Anna.

"One day in the Destramech palace, the royal fool told a joke about taking over Arigog to the King and his council. Naturally, this joke had spread across the lands like a plague. While the council thought that the joke was funny, the King thought otherwise. He thought about the idea until he was consumed with greed and decided to take action. With a large army and a small number of loyal Destramechs, the King began to expand and planned to take over Arigog. Immediately, the people of Arigog wouldn't accept this. Neither did other people, including other Destramechs. Then one night, a group of Destramechs snuck into Arigog and killed a man. The innocent man was just leaving his work to go home to his wife and family." Everyone sat in disbelief. "The people of Arigog were outraged. They began fighting, and war was declared."

"Did the Destramech family agree?"

"Even though they were loyal to Destera, they refused to accept the King's new ideas. So they left the land, saying that they should return in a few days. Forty years came and went before the war ended. But when it did, there was emptiness and cold-heartedness, not just in Arigog and Destera, but in all of the lands. Places where there were battles were reduced to nothing, homes were left in flames, and so much blood was shed. So . . . much . . . blood."

"What happened to the Destramechs after the war ended?" asked Amelia.

"They went back to Destera and built a wall. The wall is so tall that you can only see the castle fully if you were at a faraway distance."

"And what happened to the Destramech family?"

"They never came back. My great-grandfather was worried and tried repeatedly to find them, only to end up being unsuccessful. My great-grandfather . . . my grandmother . . . they died knowing that there were good Destramechs. I believe that my family is with them right now and my grandmother is playing with her friend."

"What was her friend's name?"

"Deidra."

An hour passed as everyone was getting tired. As Mila laid her head down, she stopped and jumped out of her bed. "The battle is over," she said.

"Yes," said Murean, "We know that."

"But we've won."

"Yes, dear. We know that, too."

"We can get out of here."

Everyone then popped up out of bed in realization. "She's right," said Anna, "we can escape . . . Arugh!" Anna tried to get up, but the pain in her side pulled her back down.

"Stay down," said Edith as she helped Anna to sit back down. "You are too hurt to move."

"But . . . but . . . I have to... Arugh!" She tried to get up again, only to end up in painful failure. "I . . . I guess you're right. You all . . . need to . . . to leave me."

"What?"

"I can't move. I'll only slow you guys down."

"But you are our leader."

"And as leader, I need you all to leave me behind. I'm sure you all can go on without me."

"We cannot," said Amelia. "We will not. Not without you. It is either all of us or none of us. We are staying together."

Everyone nodded their heads in agreement.

Anna, who knew that there was no chance in persuading them otherwise, just sighed and said, "You all are taking a great risk just to be with me."

"Not really," said Murean, "there isn't a map that could get us out of here anyway."

After a moment of silence, Tama asked, "Weren't we supposed to burn the bodies?" Everyone except for Anna and Mila jumped out of bed and ran outside.

"Hold on there, Delilah," called Anna. "You're supposed to stay inside."

"Oh . . . right . . . of course." Delilah then went back inside and closed the tent flap.

Chapter 19:

The Interrogation

Amelia and the other slaves rushed to the spot where the bodies were piled up. A cold breeze filled the air, and there were patches of grass and snow that were stained in blood.

"Where are the bodies?" asked Amelia. The once large pile of corpses had disappeared, and the ground looked as if it had been moved. "The hunters must have buried them. Where are they?"

"In the dining tent," said Murean. The dining tent was lit inside and was indeed filled with hunters.

Amelia reached for the tent flap, but it opened, and Master Jack stood on the other side. "You're supposed to be in your tent."

"Forgive us," said Amelia, "but we were supposed to burn the bodies."

"We're having the bodies burned outside of the camp already. Instead, you all can make yourselves useful and put away the stuff at the kitchen tent." Everyone began to walk away, but Jack quickly grabbed Amelia. "Get me some water."

"Yes, sir." Amelia ran with the others.

There, next to the kitchen tent, were stacks of objects. There were large sacks of food, new pots and pans, jars of oils and spices, new dishes, and wrapped up meats and cheeses.

"This will last us for months," said Edith, who stood there in awe. While the others were unpacking, Amelia took a cup of water and went back to the dining tent. Inside, the men were standing in a big huddle while Master Jack was sitting on top of a new table.

"Thank you," he said as he took a sip.

Curious about what the hunters were doing, Amelia crept behind the huddle, which was now breaking apart. Inside the huddle was the caped soldier that Jack struck earlier on his knees with his hands tied behind his back and his bowed head bleeding. This left Amelia quite surprised. She could have sworn that he was thrown into the pile with the other bodies. She remembers this because he was one of the few bodies whose eyes were closed. She walked over to try to retrieve the body only to look closely and realize that the man was still alive.

"Now," said sweaty Gremeak as he pulled the soldier's hair, "talk. What's your name?"

"My name," the soldier said in a sharp tone, "is Dereck Banter, son of Sir Borin Banter, second-in-command of the Violet troops, loyal citizen of Destera."

"So that's why Banter went crazy when you fell. You're his kid."

"Indeed."

"So," Gremeak said as he walked around, "what do you know? How did you find us? Are the Destramechs planning anything else?"

"I will not tell you anything."

"Tell us what you know."

"I will not."

"Tell us!"

"No!"

"Tell us, or I swear I will cut your throat and you can kiss your father goodbye!"" As Gremeak said that, he pulled out his sword and aimed it at Banter's throat. "I will happily kill you, so that way I can see the look on your father's face. He would try to sneak in and retrieve his son's body, only to find it cut up and presented with your eyes wide opened. He will stand there in tears with his head going numb. And when I've had my fun, I'll stab his skull!"

Banter's eyes first widened, and then began to show tears as he wept. Gremeak, who now looked as if he was regretting his words, lowered his sword and put it away. "This," he said softly, "was not how I wanted this to go. All we want is a little information."

"If I give you some information," he sobbed, "will you let me go?"

"Sure."

Banter then took a deep breath. "I will talk."

"Good!"

"I . . . I do have information . . ." Then he sat there in silence.

"Well," said Gremeak, "What is it?"

"I do have information . . . but I am not sure that I should say it . . ." He then sat there again in silence.

"Well, why not?"

"The Destramechs . . ."

"What about them?"

"The Destramechs . . . they will come after me . . ."

"Why?"

"For . . . for the information . . . for the information that you want me to tell you."

"Well, that won't be a pro—"

"No! No! I cannot do it! I will not tell! I will not tell!"

"It will be fine!"

Then there was silence. "Very well . . . I will talk . . ."

"All right. What is it?"

"Wait . . . I do not believe that I can tell."

"Well, sure you ca—"

"No! I will not tell! I will not tell!"

"No one will come after you if you tell!"

"Fine! I will— Arrrgh!"

Before Banter could say another word, Jack had snuck up behind him and stabbed a sword through his back. Banter screamed as blood came out of his mouth. Then he fell over, dead with eyes wide opened. Jack, who looked irritated, left the sword inside. Gremeak stared at Banter and then at Jack, trying his best to come up with the right words. "Jack! Are you . . . you must be . . . why would you do that? The boy . . . he . . . he was young! He was just about to tell us something! He could have given us a location or something! How could y—"

"How . . . could . . . I . . . what?" Jack calmly interrupted. "How could I, a man like myself, save you all a lot of time from being wasted?"

"Wasted? Jack, you didn't hear what he was saying. He said-"

"I will talk. I do have the information. Information that I should tell. But I am not sure if I should say it. The Destramechs, they will come after me for the information you want me to tell. No. No. I cannot do it. I will not tell. I will not tell."

Gremeak and the others stood there in astonishment. "How did you know?"

"I've interrogated enough Destramechs soldiers to know their little memorized act."

"Act?" asked Lance. "You mean he was faking the entire time?"

"Yes," replied Jack as he took out the sword and gave it to a hunter. "While the Destramech soldiers are trained physically, they are also trained with their words. They have been taught that if they are captured and interrogated for information, they are to say and repeat those words for as long as they can." Jack then went to the table, took another sip of water, and came back.

"But why?" asked a hunter.

"To keep themselves quiet. They say the words over and over to keep their enemies from actually knowing any information. They stall by making it seem as if they'll tell you something, then they will back out, and then they will do it again. In the end, you'll be wasting energy and time while just getting nowhere."

"And once again," said Gremeak, "you have proven yourself as the best. Well, I'm not sure for you all, but that battle wore me out. I'm going to bed."

All of the hunters murmured in agreement. They all began to leave the tent as Jack finished his water. "Slave."

"Yes, sir?"

"Take this back to the kitchen tent and go to bed."

"Yes sir." Amelia then took the cup, took one last look at Jack and walked away.

Chapter 20:

Peaceful Morning

The morning air arrived at the camp as the tired hunters went to bed and as Amelia took the empty cup out of the dining tent. As she left, the kitchen tent, to her surprise, was now right next to the dining tent. The pile of supplies was replaced with a pile of old and rusty pots, along with old food and filthy dishes. Inside, the slaves were sitting on overturned rusty pots. "What took you so long?" asked Murean as Amelia flipped a dirty pot and sat down. "Did something happen?"

"Yes. The caped soldier that Jack struck was still alive. He was being interrogated by the hunters."

"Did he tell anything?"

"No. He refused to give any information, so Master Jack killed him."

"Oh."

"Amelia?" asked Tama.

"Yes?"

"You're the Arigogian princess, right."

"Yes. That is correct."

"Then we might be free soon." Everyone looked at Tama. "Think about it. As the next line to the throne, you are one of the most important people in Arigog. Your men are probably looking for you right now, searching high and low for their lost princess."

"Yes, to take me to my death."

"Perhaps . . . or to rescue and bring you home and free us." Everyone stared at her in silence and confusion. "It was just a thought."

"Well, I think it was a . . ." Before Amelia could finish her sentence, she felt her stomach grumble. "Is . . . anyone else . . . hungry?"

"Yes," said Murean, "we haven't eaten since lunch yesterday."

"Well," said Edith, "we have a bounty of food to eat."

Amelia then looked and saw, to her surprise, a sack of delicious red apples. "Where did you get those apples?"

"They were found at the camp. There're sacks full of them."

"And we have grains . . . and cream . . . and spices . . . and honey. We can make apple tarts."

"Apple tarts?"

"Yes. I used to eat them at home. We can make them right now."

"Well, we don't have anything else to do." So everyone got up and prepared the ingredients.

Amelia remembered how Daleen did it as if it was yesterday. First, Tama peeled, cored and warmed up the apples with cream and honey. Meanwhile, Murean and Amelia made some dough with honey and added the filling. Afterward, Edith cooked them over a fire, and Amelia observed until each tart was golden brown. By the time dawn was near, they had made twenty apple tarts.

As they entered the slave tent with a large plate of the tarts, the sweet aroma filled the room and woke up the others who were sleeping inside. "What smells good?" asked Anna as she struggled to sit up.

"Apple tarts," said Edith. "They were Amelia's idea. We've made enough for all of us to have seconds and more."

Amelia came in smiling as she passed out the new plates and forks, along with cups and a pitcher of water. Edith quickly placed the hot plate on her bed and everyone carefully placed two tarts on their plates. After several minutes of letting the tarts cool down, they began to eat.

"My," said Edith, "this is delicious."

"She's right," said Anna. "This is one of the best things that I've ever had."

"It's really yummy, Amelia." said Mila with a mouthful of tarts.

Amelia, who was surprised by the compliments, stabbed her fork into the tart, closed her eyes, and took a bite. The sweet flavors of the tart brought her memories. It reminded her of when she was little, the last time she remembers being truly happy in years, tasting her first apple tart in the royal kitchen. It reminded her of being in the Revel Forest months ago, hiding under a tree in the rain next to Daleen's ugly bag and a sword that was initialed "Shaw" and "R.T.S."

But now, she's eating apple tarts as an enslaved prisoner in a camp full of bounty hunters, eating with other slaves. A slave who is a great warrior, a girl who cares about a doll more than her own life, a leader who's now too injured to move, a woman who is a great cook, a lady who is actually a Destramech, and a slave who is turning out to be a good friend. This Amelia knew without a doubt, but despite the circumstance of not being free, something felt different. It was as if something in this tent, being here, surrounded by people who actually cared about her and Amelia being able to say the same, to be free from the restrictions of a boring princess life, something about that made the tart taste even sweeter. Suddenly, Amelia felt her bed move and opened her eyes.

Murean was sitting next to her munching on her tart. "I need you to be honest with me," she whispered.

"Of course, friend."

"We are in the middle of the biggest forest in the land as slaves, surrounded by the best hunters that ever lived. Do you really think that we could escape . . . that one day we will all be free?"

"I am hoping so."

"But . . . do you believe that you will be free?"

"Well, in a way," Amelia said with a smile, "I already am."

Murean smiled back. Everyone continued to eat as they stared outside. The sun was now rising on this new day.

About the Author

Amber Turner Darby was born on June 22, 1996 in Silver Spring, Maryland. After conquering her learning challenges, she discovered her talents of Creative Writing in the 9th grade. Since then, she has written many poems, haikus and one of her three books thus far. She graduated from Riverdale Baptist School in the National Honor Society and is starting her freshman year at college in the fall of 2014. She is loved and supported by her mother, father, brother, over twelve aunts and uncles, her church family and friends.

www.ingramcontent.com/pod-product-compliance
Lightning Source LLC
Chambersburg PA
CBHW051651260626
47170CB00004B/1443